JAMEELAH RA'OOF

White SPACES

— A NOVELLA —

AUTHOR OF:

LOW PLACES: A FEARLESS TALE OF REDEMPTION

THE CRYSTAL LOCKET: A NOVEL

RE-$ET: UNCOVERING THE TRUTH BY ANY MEANS

STOP WAITING ON OTHER PEOPLE'S YES! GRATITUDE JOURNAL

STOP WATING! HOW PUTTING OFF MY DREAMS NEARLY WASTED MY LIFE

STOP WAITING! LITTLE BOOK OF AFFIRMATIONS

ISBN-13: 978-0-578-60790-0

WHITE SPACES

DEDICATION

To Humanity...

WHITE SPACES

BY JAMEELAH RA'OOF

JAMEELAH RAOOF

TABLE OF CONTENTS

JAMEELAH RAOOF

JAMEELAH RAOOF

LET'S BEGIN HERE...

I am supposed to be angry about my blackness, angry about slavery and angry at white privilege. But I am not. At least not on a personal or venomous level. Race feels like something that happens on the outside of my world, something distant, petty and lazy. I am mostly disappointed with some aspects of human behavior in general, as opposed to directing that disappointment at one race or one gender. While I recognize that I am a part of the dance whether I feel the beat of the music or not, this does not change my lack of attachment to organizing myself, my life and my existence around race.

When I stack, meaning layer myself with my prestigious labels, like educated, well-traveled, college professor, etc., it's because I want to further distance myself from everyone's cube (box) of stories, whether the onlookers are white, black, yellow or brown.

However, it is *white spaces* that dominate my environment, and white stories that flood my media and white people who are dangerously clueless about the implications of race. And since *by and large,* I am not angry, do not see whites as powerful saviors or feel as though whites are somehow better off than me simply because they are white, or view my blackness a burden to be carried laboriously, a perpetual deficit; I feel it is my duty, moreover, my responsibility to speak candidly and fearlessly about my black experience in white spaces; professional white spaces, academic white spaces, recreational white spaces and romantic white spaces. I am Yasminah, and this is my truth.

"You are not only responsible for what you say, but also for what you do not say."
~MLK

JAMEELAH RAOOF

CHAPTER ONE

My Pot Dealer

My dealer is a chick. A badass, business owning, minivan driving, pot smoking, suburban wife, mother of two kind of chick. Her daughters are in gymnastics, soccer, and dance. Rachel goes to the gym five days a week. Her self-proclaimed uniform is a waist-trainer, the latest running sneaks and skin-tight yoga gear. She has an office downtown where she services upper-class, stay-at-home moms as a massage therapist. It's complete with a childcare space, receptionist and a safe that holds her stash. Her stash of edible pot snacks, hydroponic weed, and high-end waist-trainers. Like I said, she is a badass. I visit her once a month, rarely at her business. Early on we discover that she lives closer to me than she does to her office, so once a month we meet at a gas station nestled between a busy intersection and the interstate. Rachel is bubbly and sweet with honest eyes and a nurturing warmth. The meets are transactional: I pay her fifty dollars and she gives me an old school sandwich bag of carefully measured, "regular" weed. Since I am weening myself off both Lexapro and Xanax, she is my pharmacist and my savior.

I am also a soccer mom, heavily educated, well-employed; but I'm divorced, and she is not. I am referred to her by a friend of a friend. The conversation to ask for a dealer is awkward. That's the problem with being a mature, upstanding (mostly law-abiding) citizen, you tend not to know anyone willing to be upfront about their vices. When one of my exes sold weed, many of his clients were women like me. They liked him because he had a home and kids and he wasn't rough around the edges. They could trust him. He was approachable, excellent at code-switching, able to communicate with hood folks on the weekend and do his corporate job during the week. He was the last person that regularly supplied me. Along with the dissolution of our relationship also went my direct connection to that leafy godsend, hence the Lexapro and the Xanax.

In the pot world, you never want to look or act like you're addicted. You're supposed to be easy about it. If you have it, that's good, but if you don't that's good too. It's not crack after all. Therefor mentioning to a friend that you need a hookup, even if she partakes herself, must be done in a delicate manner. Like, *give me your dealer's name if you want, I mean, I don't really care...I mean like whatever...I have other people I can ask...* Both parties usually understand this attitude to be a lie, but this is an unspoken rule, you don't act like a crackhead no matter how addicted you are, no matter how many withdrawal symptoms you're experiencing. Like, loss of appetite, extreme anxiety, insomnia, depression, lack of sexual desire.

It's funny because all the great side effects are; improved appetite, calmed nerves, sound sleep, happiness and an amped up sex drive. But when you don't get your fix, all the fun parts are taken away three times over. It's like the universe says, with a wicked but loving tone, *ha ha ha, you thought you could trick universal law...well I've got your number...ha ha ha...*

The first time me and Rachel meet it feels more like a book club gathering. I pull into the busy gas station and my paranoia sets in. I take myself very seriously. I don't like making mistakes and I often joke with people that I wish I were a robot, since being human for me is sometimes painful. I am pragmatic. In a therapy session, I attended during my marriage, I was told that I had fishbowl mentality, meaning that I treat life as if someone is always watching, watching and judging. The therapist even guessed that I don't like to urinate in public stalls if others are around and can hear the trickle. He was right. I need to be on my best behavior at all times.

Rachel is already sitting at a pump at the far end of the station. I recognize her vehicle through a short description given in her text message. The sun is bright, and the bustle of the busy city is loud. I roll down my window about halfway. I want to get a feel for what is happening around me without being incubated. Hearing the cars, the people, the wind, is neutralizing, calming.

Another rule to interacting with a dealer is to not use too many words. My ex used few words. So few, it was sometimes hard for me to follow him. A dealer is expected to exude a coolness that belies the need for wordy exchanges. I park at the pump parallel to her. Rachel catches a glimpse of my searching eyes and a large smile grows on her face. As soon as my car is in park, she is already hopping out of her van and into my passenger seat. She immediately wraps me in a warm, friendly hug and says, "Hi, I'm Rachel".

She has deep brown skin, that glows as bright as her smile, a shapely physique, and an unassuming nature. "Hi, Yasminah." I reply feeling a shyness propelled further by her unwavering confidence.

She asks me how my day has been. We share a few words about our mutual connection, who is another (mostly) stay-at-home mom; meaning, we work outside of the house but can be home whenever we choose. Rachel goes on to ask me what I do for a living and whether I enjoy it. I feel welcomed. I exhale thanking the law of attraction for sending me such an awesome dealer. I don't have to try with her. I'm so accustomed to trying everywhere I go that her focus on my comfort takes me by surprise. It's like she knows her niche and how to accommodate their bashfulness.

We establish a bond through discussing our children, our workout routines, our hopes and aspirations. The transaction is our last topic of discussion. Rachel is classy, she knows people and she knows, it seems, a little bit about everything. She has cultural capital, a renaissance woman if you will. I love this. Who says a dealer should be seedy? She reads off my purchasing options like the server at a bistro reads a menu, learning the most prized items by heart. She even makes the proper facial expression for the items that are in highest demand. I tell her I just want regular weed. She smiles and hands over a little box of what looks like a ten pack of grape flavored, Kool-Aid water sweeteners. I assume the little carton is a front. After I hand over my fifty dollars, Rachel doesn't count it, she slips it straight into her pocket. It's clear she's not needy about making a sale. She chooses to provide a service that you can either take or leave.

Just before we wrap up our conversation, she pulls out her phone and shows me pictures of her babies, who are half-white. I wonder if she shows them for that reason or just to dote, I choose to believe it's the latter.

We part ways with no empty plans to communicate outside of my requests. She hands me her business card for massage therapy and I drive away. I drive away on a high, from such a beautiful, breezy exchange. I relish it for a moment.

It wasn't until I made it home that I checked the box. I screech, "yesss!" I am beyond stoked. I have learned to acquire my own fix, without the use of my ex. For me, this small victory solidifies my independence. I start to feel I don't even need it. But of course, I smoke it anyway.

JAMEELAH RAOOF

CHAPTER TWO

White Spaces

Race is in America is an obsession. A pastime. A sport. A tool. Both a social experience and experiment. The only thing America is more obsessed with than race is beauty. It is common to hear among successful black women that they are often the only black woman in the board room. Hearing about that position and being it are two wholly different states of affairs. Yoga, soccer, ballet, grad school, my neighborhood, my job, the company Christmas party and host of other places; these are my white spaces. As poised as I like to think I am, when I find myself in these spaces, which is often, I'm quite self-conscious. Although, I appear the opposite.

I am asked frequently what I do for a living. They want to know my secret to infiltrating white spaces. They study both me and my children. They seem unsure of my smile. *Is it the same smile as a white woman's? Or does a black woman's smile inherently mean something different?* Sometimes there are other races and ethnicities present, but just as I, they have been covered with the same confining blanket of whiteness. Theses spaces exude prestige and exclusivity but are more common than not, harmless. The worst-case scenarios are generally only in my mind.

Privileged spaces have pristine facilities; modern yoga studios, green parks, well-stocked grocery stores, no vagabonds and spotless streets. It's not as much about whiteness, as it is about what whiteness provides. I'd never want to be anything other than that only black woman in the room. I adore it and fear it at the same time. Like I adore my children but fear losing them all in one thought. I refuse to allow my skin color to dictate my choices. I don't teach this to my daughters and neither do I participate in self-inflicted segregation. I do not abhor white spaces, for me, they just *are*.

On no particular afternoon, late one summer, I walk into a new yoga studio. I found it online after deciding that I could not trick myself into any fitness challenge on my own terms at home. Each session that was intended to be an hour long mostly ended after ten or fifteen minutes. I don't have the discipline to practice alone. I left my last studio after being a member for four years. It was an all-white space. I was both visible and invisible. They rarely made full eye contact and barely used my name. Once one instructor referred to me as "pumpkin head" instead of asking me how to pronounce Yasminah. This might have been no big deal, had I not been a member for three years and seeing her at least four days a week. I am intimidated by their world and they seem intimidated by me. I am tall, slender, muscular, flexible, all the requirements to be a member of the in-crowd. I hold short conversations every now and again, but I am black. They see me as that first.

I don't mind being the black girl as much as they mind that they cannot forget that I am her. That feeling is awkward. It is always awkward since there is nothing I can do to put them at ease but disappear. I leave the studio, not because of those silly infractions, I leave because my journey there is over. The new studio has my attention because they offer childcare. I arrive one afternoon to vet the place, first for my children's comfort and second for my own.

My daughters peek into the space with clear discernment. They are choosy. My girls do not understand the feeling of unwantedness.

As much as society insists on teaching them that they are the "other", they do not feel this. I cushion their exposure by never watching the news or any programs that suggest people who look like them are less than. I am fully aware this ideal is programmed into my country's DNA. Racial hierarchies are entrenched in the depths of its soul and are ceremoniously cultivated through both intention and ignorance. Racism is in the air, the water and the earth. I do my best to show them that they are wanted, that they are important. And that they matter, to me, unconditionally.

My daughters know their value like the way they know they have long hair and that they are sisters. Their self-worth is embedded. They scan the room like little meticulous prim donnas. They never consider for one moment that I would leave them in the childcare if they don't like the way it feels. The oldest exhales. The youngest looks over at her big sister, then she exhales too. They hug me around my waist. This process is silent. I don't try to nudge them either way. I want them to feel that their instincts matter too.

To be honest, I don't know what white women think of me. I don't care to assume. I just know that their reception with each other is relaxed and with me, its uneasy and often apologetic. Too attentive. This new studio is beautiful, tall ceilings, glossy bamboo floors and windows that allow the sun to pour over every inch of the room.

I feel small here, but not like low self-worth or low self-esteem or not good enough small. I feel packaged, contained, like my story has been told for me before I utter a word. I feel my experiences, though unique, are not considered and I am politely placed into a small cube of blackness. It's so tight in this space, it's so hard to be free in this space. My freedom does not look the same as their freedom. My self-esteem does not feel the same as their self-esteem. My self-esteem is in spite of.

I envy their privilege of blank pages, of story creating. Of being on the inside of conversations about themselves. There is nothing like being in a white space and sitting in on conversations about yourself, as a black woman, without being included. This is what it feels like when I watch movies or read books about black women but not of black women. Most times I occupy merely the reception of a story that has been told for me, long before I arrived.

Its often a double-edged sword. I have no desire to speak for all black women, but I do understand that my perspective is needed, desired and required, especially in these spaces.

I don't envy their whiteness, I envy their privilege in white spaces. I envy the perception that they have money, that they are educated, that they have husbands if they have children in tow. I stack my education on top of my small, black cube, I stack my "have been married" on top of my education, and on top of that; I stack with my Range Rover, being a college professor and a world traveler. I stack high. I stack high enough to stand on top of it all. To stand tall enough to beyond belong, tall enough to be better. I love to be better. Especially in white spaces. Once I mentally stack, I can breathe, I have freedom. I am far above the fray. I am existing at a higher altitude, where breathing is easy, and the population is sparse. The pilot has turned off the seatbelt light and I am free to move about the cabin. Now...now we can start yoga.

It is often said that there is no such thing as being good at yoga. This is true, but I am good at yoga. I am great at yoga actually. I pose well, but not just that, yoga speaks to me. Yoga in big cities is governed by white spaces, expensive white spaces. I call them the Lululemon crowd. The crowd that does not see the studio as a quiet sanctuary where their complaints about married life, their children or how the lawn guy missed a spot, should not enter. This use to annoy me, but I am so good at yoga that I know how to block them out. I am good at yoga because I have patience for my slow growth there. I don't need to have it all today in yoga, it's a forward, slow progression that feels like home to me. It feels like my favorite blanket with the large print of a unicorn on it, has been dragged with me into this space. I am not inhibited here. I don't over think trying and falling. I play on the insecurity of the other women who are afraid to even try.

It's like their fear is energetic power and I suck it up like a super hero that drains the energy of others to use for their own mighty agenda. I float above the room, handstands, arm balances, headstands, etc. My legs are long, my arms are muscular, and I just look better doing yoga than most. I know this, and I pretend like I don't. I am told, "You have a beautiful practice..." "Oh thank you..." I say, but I think, "I know." I smile. Although I mostly stack my cube in my head, it still works.

I go to grad school and this process of stacking starts all over again. I am addicted to being better. It might have begun as over-compensation but now it just feels good. I don't feel guilty for feeling good about being better than others at things.

In the academic white space, I thought I could not cut it. I fall for the story I have been fed. Sometimes I stuff myself into that cube before anyone else has the chance. Imposter syndrome. I think I don't deserve to be there and then one day, out of the blue, I'm asked to be an associate instructor by my department head. Dr. Grey is a white woman, fifty to sixty years old with a twelve-year-old son. She is tenured and claims that if she had her son any earlier she would likely not have been offered her position. She speaks often about the glass ceiling and female leadership. This is both our bridge and divide. I feel black women have always been leaders and taking a backseat to a more successful husband has not historically been a common option. I don't always connect with her feminism talk. She not only teaches statistics, but she loves to analyze them. Most statisticians only see the numbers, but Dr. Grey sees the stories behind them.

In her class, each time statistics related to race are used I challenge any that speak negatively toward my blackness. I don't even defend my womanhood the way I defend my blackness. The subject of black people is invisible unless we discuss poverty, crime, single motherhood or prison. I ask my classmates, all white, to imagine only being summoned by society on these matters alone. They stare blankly.

After a heated discussion in class about the fate of children from single mother households, Dr. Grey pulls me aside. She speaks to me only a few inches from my face, *a white space thing*. "What do think about being a TA?" She asks, titling her head in as if she were delivering the details of a covert CIA operation. I pivot to clear some space between our lips. I say yes instantly. This makes me wonder how she sees me. *Is this white guilt or does she see me? Does she see my wealth?*

As a TA, I am asked to complete menial tasks for three instructors. I had only started the program a semester before and vowed I would finish in only a year. I am encouraged by my professors not to take so many classes. *Is this because they don't think I can cut it?* I never know what to think. I never know what story is on the table. This consumes me, until I stack. For me, stacking is a drug. Better than pot. I stack to control my narrative. While I take myself seriously, I understand that I am not my accomplishments, but they *are* nestled in with me everywhere I go. They help me breathe. They gobble up my insecurities and my anxiety. I am in love with my accomplishments, for this reason alone. Men don't make me feel the way success does. I school the whole summer and finish in one year. Yep, I am better.

~

Being submerged in these spaces didn't start for me as an adult. My neighborhood growing up was a white space, which the neighbors made clear by displaying meticulously placed black, red and white lawn jockeys, whose sole purpose was to mind their yards. Like garden gnomes, these little non-threatening black men were decoration, fodder, not neighbors.

In middle school I'm thrust into honors classes because of my natural academic abilities. Everyone is white, except for two Asian kids. These classes are quieter than my old ones. There are actual expectations, even the teacher is more focused and involved. I don't notice that my black is noticed or even cared about with my classmates. I ignore race. Not because I had been taught to. Quite the opposite.

Both my parents are former Nation of Islam members, led the by honorable Warith Dean Mohammed. In my childhood home we are taught pride to be the descendants of "cotton pickers and field niggers". They speak about the resilience, forgiveness and grit my ancestors possessed, and how slaves saved America's humanity. I hold no shame in my blackness. Books on our shelves tell stories of black inventors and political heroes. They knw our history books are white spaces, so they carve out a new space for us and people like us at home. I'm not taught to dislike whites or to hate them. On the contrary, I'm taught to feel sorry for them. My parents stack very high at home. I stand on the stacks they provide, before I learn to create my own. By the time I face the world, it is hard to find people who I think are better than me. I learn early to leap beyond everyone with my intellect and this includes whites. They were not exempt are surmountable.

I have a party for my twelfth birthday and invite all my honors classmates. Only the black girls from my old, non-honors classes show up. I learn that my home, no matter how big and nice it is, it is not big enough to hold white space.

I ignore race for the better half of my life. My intellect opens doors for me. I don't know how to be angry about being black. It seems I am never sad enough about being black to fit into black spaces or white spaces. My attitude is an anomaly. The world doesn't like anomalies. It doesn't know where to put them. The world is hell bent on knowing what cube to stick me into. What story best suits me based on first and foremost, my race. I don't learn until I'm nearly eighteen years old that black people only make up roughly twelve percent of the population of the United States. My brother delivers this morsel of knowledge during a conversation about race. I say, "Isn't it like fifty-fifty...blacks and whites?" He smirks. He is happy to bring some alarming, earth-shattering news to baby sister. "No..." he replies. He shares the stats. Growing up in black spaces like the black Muslim community, and in New Orleans itself, had skewed my thinking. I think, *how did I miss that all through school?* I think I know enough about the history of my country to ignore the present. Race to me, feels like history. It never occurs to me that being black could hinder my present.

I create my own privilege with my intellect. My assumption is that because I make privilege with my intellect, all those who inherently make up privileged white spaces do the same. *They couldn't be experiencing privilege just because they're white?*

In academia I began to grow secretly bitter that I have to work so hard to gain the baseline of acknowledgement that is given so freely to white women, no matter their intellect. White women control and govern all the opportunities I am graciously given throughout my academic career. Their language, their hair, their thinness, their concerns, their belief that their experiences are universal; all serve as gatekeepers. White women are my gatekeepers. This is a hard pill to swallow.

I am forced to notice race and I don't like it. It feels like floating on my back in a body of water, and suddenly noticing I've floated too far away from the shore, and I can no longer feel the bottom. In academia, I am forced to realize that I can no longer feel the bottom. When I get deep inside these spaces I realize these gatekeepers aren't that smart. Their whiteness has acted for them, as a giant cube of goodies. Their connections, their upper-middle classness and sameness drives their promotion. It does not limit their story, but instead it expands it far beyond their own reach.

My brilliance shock and intimidate all in one swoop. I grow tired of shocking and intimidating. Overtime, I learn not to stack so high in order to put others at ease. I infiltrate these spaces all throughout my adulthood because this is where the better stuff is. This is where the better opportunities are. This is where it is quiet and peaceful and where growth is expected, it is wide-open even for a brown woman, as long as she is clever. She may have to be stealthy, but she has room. There is always room for a few brown women that understand their culture, hierarchies and beliefs; even if she does not ascribe to them herself. I understand I must leave any bitterness and anger at home. I have to teeter between eagerness and gratitude but never aggressiveness. My aggressive is not the same as a white woman's aggressive. My aggressive needs to be punished, scolded and put in its place. Her aggressive is often referred to as feminism, girl power, breaking the glass ceiling.

~

I find a house for my young family in a relatively small suburb outside of Dallas. I view the house a few times before I drag my then husband, kicking and screaming to agree on this space. It does not occur to me that it is a white space. The neighbors are very tight knit. All but one neighbor is skeptical of us. I renovate the house inside and out. I cut bushes, tame the landscaping, plant flowers, make shutters. In a matter of a few months our home is the best on the block. The black home in the white space is better. This makes my mother proud. "They can't say you don't keep up your house," she says. She casually points out the flaws in the white homes. What I'm not okay with is being seen as less. Less hurts, less makes me cringe, less pisses me

off, black spaces and black people, to them,
commonly are less.

CHAPTER THREE

Me

After my divorce a few years earlier, I am free. I am not perfect, but I am indeed free. When I hear people cackle about how hard marriage and kids are I want to chime in and say, "the kids are easy without the marriage". But I know this is not the experience of many. I know I'm supposed to drudge about referring to myself as a single mom; two of the least appreciated statuses in our society, single and mom. I am both of these things, and I am also infinitely so much more. I bounce through a series of losers right after my decree is signed. The first guy was clearly a wife beater, whom I met in an anger management class I was banished to during my divorce. The judge put me in the corner. I am punished for being angry about my poor choices. The second guy I met in Target and in hindsight, he may have been shoplifting. After a few peculiar meetings; that felt more like me picking him up from some obscure location for a ride home, I began to wonder if he is a crackhead. Actually, I'm sure he was a young crackhead. The next time around I am convinced that online dating would put me back in my comfort zone. A relationship. The quality of said relationship was not on the table, just a relationship would do.

I was always open to other races and ethnicities of men. He never *had* to be black. They just mostly were. When I make my profile, I check the non-discriminant racial box. I load pictures of my sleek figure with visible cleavage. Moments later my inbox runneth over. I had been with one man for seven years, so this is exciting. I mostly talk to men through text and over the phone. I ignore their calls like a mac in training. I feel in charge. It's not long before I meet Rogelio. He is Mexican, educated, employed and a father of one. That one being a one month old. I tell myself that there's nothing wrong with a man on a dating site who has a baby that's less than five weeks old. At least he's honest.

At the time, I had scarcity mentality when it came to dating. I am convinced Rogelio is a valid option. We click. We converse. We go to clubs. We have sex and then...and then... he runs cold. This makes me sick, not angry, just sad. I am tired of getting it wrong, I want him as validation that I can pick right. Before running cold, he asked me if I would like to take a trip to Puerto Rico with him. He said I only need to pay for my plane ticket and everything else would be taken care of. I think, *this is it, this is my dude.* This can work. I can move him in, Rogelio can help with the bills and I will help raise his one month old. In hindsight, thank God for prayers that are never answered.

No matter how hopeless this looks, I'm convinced that I can't trust myself. I get attached. I began to yearn his calls, complain about his text message turn-around time to anyone who listens. I fall directly into the patterns I fell into with my children's father. I give away all my power. I pack it in a box, buy postage and ship it off with no return to sender. I don't know how to not do this. I come from a family full of strong women and no happy marriages. I blame my choices on this. I decide to go to Puerto Rico with Rogelio. This all happens in three short weeks.

Of course, Puerto Rico is amazing. Rogelio and I grow even more attached. I ignore the slow fade treatment I was given before the trip. Ghosting, is what they call it. The sex is not spectacular, but it *is* worth my time. We stay in a condo, on the fifth floor, overlooking the main avenue in front of the beach. The ocean is beautiful. We jump waves and I do my best to act secure. I am a nervous wreck the whole time. I want to own him, and this feeling of wanting for the future is ruining my present. I panic because he is not attached like me and I can feel it. After our trip, we fizzle out. I think, *my family is right.* I don't know how to pick, men always leave or stay and hurt me. My heart is broken. Not over Rogelio, but over believing that I could find the love of my life on a dating app. I'm angry about this. I'm angry about love. I'm angry about everything so I puff on my pot even more. *I'm so stupid,* I think.

This time I take a real break. This is when I begin to truly indulge my daughters. I make family rules. I blog about not seeing being divorced as negative and I write a list of twenty-five great things about being single. I believe wholeheartedly in this list. I decide that relationships are not fulfilling, they cannot complete me and that I will never lift another finger to keep a man's attention. I will not pretend. I will smoke my pot, got to work, raise my kids do yoga and travel the world.

I can believe in myself in yoga. I lay in sivasana after each class, loving myself, trusting myself. This does not depend on anyone else's opinion of me, only what I feel about myself. And most times I know what I feel isn't always true either. I dive into love with me, I dive into love with my daughters. I never come up for air.

Nearly a year has gone by since Rogelio and I bid each other adieu. He makes weak efforts to return but the thrill is gone. We both know it. Like the tremors after the big earthquake, you want to get excited by the movement, but you know the big one has already come and gone. Puerto Rico was our earthquake.

After one too many tokes, I sit quietly while the girls are visiting family and the inspiration hits me to make another online dating profile. After all, I'm invincible now. I have something. I have my love for myself, I have yoga, I have my career, I have my experiences and I have my babies. "You're the best mommy in the world," they say out of the blue, all the time, like two little fairies fluttering in my midst, dropping pixie dust on my nose until I giggle with delight. Men are an afterthought, purely entertainment. I get it this time. I swear to myself that I get it. I am determined to learn how to date without expectations. I am determined to be choosy. I choose them, they don't get to choose me. I create my profile, this time with all truths, meaning no cleavage and short skirts. I leave that to those other kinds of women. I might be the kind of woman that allegedly tried to run her ex over with a car but a hooch, I am not.

My yoga studio is a hotbed for sexy white guys. I never notice white men as viable long-term options until yoga. I notice them notice me and suddenly a light goes off. A new world inside of me awakes. I want to traverse the terrain, climb the mountains and swim in the sea. *White men*, I think, *how exciting*. I begin to pay close attention to interracial couples, how they look at each other, how they hold hands, how they eat out together. A friend tells me that, everything that black women actually are on the inside; strong, resilient, intelligent and clever, white men are seen as being on the outside, whether they truly possess those characteristics or not. Historically, black women have not endured a male counterpart who wielded more power than her. Historically, she has watched her male counterpart be stripped of power. This makes for a very different kind of woman. I try not to create a cube for white men of my own. It's not like they would even notice my cube or my preconceived notions. They have blind confidence. White men get to be everything and nothing, without losing anything. I admire this.

I meet a few men online. White guys. I try to seem worldly and open to dating whomever. Like, been there done that. They are all really into outdoor activities, hiking, skiing, camping, mudding, floating rivers, and on and on. All of which, I don't do, and have no plans of doing so.

After nearly a week back on the dating site I get a new message. It turns out, without cleavage showing the inbox doesn't runneth over as quickly. But this is good. Less is more. More is better. Suddenly my dating pool feels infinite. "White men", I say to myself. Yes, "white men". I tremble with excitement. This is like scouring the menu at a fancy restaurant and having no luck finding what it is you want, then inconspicuously the waitress leans in and whispers, "white men...white men are also on the menu." There are so many white men. As my brother reminded me, they comprise the clear majority of men in this country. When I consider them, suddenly I can breathe. That old cube is not big enough for me. A white man can double my stack, he can stack for me. He can rescue me from that tiny cube faster than any amount of education, any amount of accomplishments and any amount of world travel. A white man is a stack in and of itself. This is not my rule.

CHAPTER FOUR

Danny Ray Austin

This is my first date with this kind of white man. He is *white-white*. No hip-hop music, trendy hood clothes or undercover adoration of black-American culture. I'm not convinced this means better, but I am convinced that this territory deserves some exploration. Maybe even conquering.

We message back and forth a few times before he asks to connect offline. I am hesitant, as I always am with online guys. I give him my number through the dating app and my phone rings in less than a minute. I jump. In moments, he morphs from 1s and 0s into a real person. His voice is both high-pitched and rugged. He tells me he is out of town doing some work for the railroad. I feel relief that I won't be asked to meet right away. He mostly rambles, and I listen.

"Top Golf!" Danny shouts in the middle of our conversation.

"What?" I ask.

"Top Golf...do you want to go to Top Golf?" his tone a bit higher this time.

I think, *what in the hell is that?* While simultaneously replying, "Sure." *Sounds like a white thing,* I think. I Google, and it is.

Golf. I show up. Beautiful and poised. Danny Ray is tall and beautiful too. Simple, black shoes, black shirt and creased jeans on bowed legs. And me, a little blue dress, flat sandals, tucked hair and not visibly nervous. The night is cool, breezy and full of early summer excitement, a lofty anticipation for the next hundred days. Summer bears witness to love in a way no other seasons experience it. The warm, humid evenings are littered with a scrumptious dose of hope and bliss. A perfect setting for the tunnel vision approach to happiness.

"Hey girl!" Danny says, like he's met me before this night, like he knows me. I smile, not smitten off the bat, but taken aback by the jaggedness of his edges. *Is he the man for me?* I think, *oh stop Yasminah.*

We go through several rounds of him attempting to pronounce my name. It morphs from yas-main-uh to jazz-mee-nuh. Danny Ray's accent prevents him from nailing it.

He talks to me like an old friend. Nothing impressive, no romance, no flowers, just friendly and easy. Top Golf is equipped with several stations for individual parties, similar to a bowling alley. Danny chooses my club. He is already settled in at our station, which looks out towards a large putting green with color-coded targets. I'm not afraid of losing his interest like I have been in the past, or was with Rogelio, his interest never seems contingent upon my display. As I swing my club ferociously, he quietly, looks deeper. I observe him observing me.

Danny Ray is outgoing, a people person, both nonchalant and eager. He talks a lot about being a railroader. He says railroader like he's a coal miner. Like the job is heavy, not just the work but carrying the guilt of dreams that are dying the worker bee death even as we small talk. Danny Ray doesn't seem proud of his title, but he does seem proud of himself in general.

We both over use the term African-American as we describe black people we know who are players in our stories.

"There's an African-American crew, a Mexican crew and the rest of the crews are white... I won't lie, the Black crew is seen as the laziest." Danny rambles, noticing his words afterwards. "I hope that doesn't offend you, I'm just talking about the job."

"Does the Black crew get paid the same as your crew?" I ask, not vested enough to discuss the psychological aspect of why them being lazy is his perception.

"Probably not..." Danny swings his club at the air right next to the ball. He is happy to leave this conversation without resolution. But I enjoy making him responsible for the full scope of his words.

"Then they probably work at the exact proportion to their pay..." I add. He hunches his shoulders, as if in consideration of my perspective.

The term African-American always seems too clunky for me, like an awkward afterthought. It is an interesting concept to be named by the dominant group in society; I'm told I'm African-American, I'm shown images I don't control, I am molded by white perception in every area of my life whether I accept it or not. I prefer Black, even though, as a word, its tied to so many negatives. It feels strong, sleek, resilient and empowered. African-American feels contrived. I guess this is why my parents gave us both Muslim first and last names, it was very important to them not to go through life with slave-master names, or to pass those names down for yet another generation. Names can restrict or create freedom. There is so much freedom in naming yourself. I figure this is why Blacks in America make up names so often, it solidifies their freedom to do so. I mean, how many Johns and Janes does the world really need?

Danny Ray's whiteness is intriguing because it's not the same. Nothing is the same about him. Not better or worse, just not the same as anyone in my past. My past is cluttered, hypocritical and heavy. Some flashbacks literally wobble my knees and shorten my breath. I inhale deep, to clear those thoughts when they arrive, like how the ocean washes away footprints, sand castles and all of yesterday's memories. In yoga we call it ujjayi breath. That's the breath I use when my past chokes me and leaves me dumbfounded.

There were some okay guys, just a few. Less than ten. With each, some lesson about who I am floating to the surface before the relationships' inevitable but not always anticipated crash and burn. *What's wrong with me? Why doesn't he like me? I thought he cared about me. I'm such a fool.* I could write a song. Several songs. I could master melancholy like Nina Simone or Phyllis Hyman. Those men are my truths, so I use the memories of them from time to time. I give them details that feel good. I cater to my happiness with them. Not my pain.

Danny Ray and I dish out a contrast that slices right through the thickest of crowds. I enjoy being different, the mystique is such a high. The center of attention without lifting a finger, only the corners of our mouths. We exhaust ourselves with banter and putt-putt, then we exhaust ourselves once more with banter and food. There is no mistaking Danny for anything more than a mustang. Wild and free. And no mistaking me for anything but an intellectual. My freedom is attached to my time, my lovemaking and my wardrobe. Everything else, uptight. Nonchalantly uptight.

He explains to me that the railroad is not his dream, but that he was never taught to have one. Danny goes on about his father. "Mean son of a bitch, never had nothing good to say to anybody," he says. Danny's eyes shift like a kid caught with his hand in the cookie jar. I sit quiet, taking in what I can use and leaving the rest behind. He turns the queries to me. I don't judge him, but I know he's not together. Something's not together. But it doesn't scare me. I welcome the opportunity to observe whatever it is that would eventually show itself to be ragged in his life. The tattered stuff.

Danny's eyes are an icy blue, like the ocean waters off Maui. They don't seduce me; culturally blue eyes and blond hair aren't at the top of my must haves list. He puts me in mind of Terry Serpico. Wrinkly forehead and all. Gruff.

"So, what's your vice?" Danny gulps his beer.

"Vice?" I shudder. I want to say, *who does he think he is?* but instead I open. My eyes vacillate just seconds before my words float into the atmosphere. His eagerness doesn't allow space for my hesitation.

"You smoke?" he asks. I frown a bit then utter, "Smoke what?"

I hold nothing back since I see no future because we are so different. I don't fidget, wonder if he likes me or flirt. I'm just there. He smiles as if to say, the night is finally getting good, she has a wild side. I chuckle, "Pot." His grin gets wider, wide enough to see his Podunk heritage. All that's missing is a piece of chewed straw hanging over his lips. It's a goofy smile like David Letterman. Like Mr. Letterman, he cleans up enough to be considered handsome. Danny Ray is quite handsome.

"Pot helps me relax," I confess.

"Darling you ain't gotta explain nothing to me." He interjects, using my confession as an invitation to take it easier than he had been. He asks the bartender for another Coors light. He's no longer with some pretentious college professor, but instead a hip chick, even younger seeming to him. He has more than three beers but less than five. He isn't driving me, so I don't keep count.

We end the night around two in the morning. I'm a good conversationalist so I rarely gauge my interest in someone based on how much conversation is had. It's too easy for me. It doesn't feel like a date, but instead a moment with a stranger, a meeting. Like the IT guys I've worked with. I have a long history with white men, but not romantically. Barely romantically anyway. He doesn't feel like a stranger, but I know he is. I am attracted to white men but from afar and a different kind than Danny Ray.

He walks me to my car, which after one glass of wine, I'd forgotten the location of. We trek all the way to the back of the lot, then back to the front. Still bantering about everything and nothing. I wonder if he wonders about my blackness or if he is more familiar than he seems. I can never figure people out these days, they're so eclectic, especially in Dallas. It's common to find out that the stiff and stuffy English professor who offices across from you at work, also moonlights as a saxophonist at a jazz club on the weekends. Very common. Don't judge a book by its cover. I Love clichés with a capitol L. They are profound and only repetition has stripped away the weight of their meaning.

The parking lot is well lit. I stand there trying to make sense of the night, trying to categorize it but I walk away just feeling that it's different, and Danny Ray is charming enough. Both different and charming, I like him, but I don't want to date him.

I have a list. It's both thorough and limited. With all the intricate nooks and crannies people possess, how can my list measure up? Danny Ray swears quite a bit, but says he's working on it. He drinks quite a bit but seems to be able to handle it. He's louder than I like, but I take inventory of the room and I'm the only one who seems bothered, unless they too are nonchalantly uptight.

I contemplate Love that night. Under the tinted reflection of moon, in that parking lot, surrounded by people sprinkled both far and near. I gaze into Danny Ray's sparkling blue eyes and I try to feel. Inhale, exhale, inhale and exhale. I feel nothing, but I like him as a person. Whatever that means. I'm happy a personality like his exists. At six feet and one inch tall, he's a lean, mean cross-fitting machine. Confidence comes easy to Danny Ray, while so many other qualities do not, and these other qualities don't exist to him.

I believe in the Law of Attraction. At this time, I had possibly taken a break from that belief in search of my other half, using an online tool nonetheless. They message, I ignore, they message again, I still ignore. I'm nice enough, but I'm sure they think I should be nicer. Its repetitive. *I'm a great guy, easy-going, laid back, still trying to find Mrs. Right, is she out there?* I'm all for internet dating. People can bump into each other online the same as they can in a bar. Like computer network collisions. We're all just data, moving from one node to the next, connecting and releasing. Collisions, the result of two devices on the same network attempting to transmit data at the same time. We're all just a bunch of collisions waiting to happen so why not collide on the information highway?

Online dating is a breeze. You create an account, post some attractive pictures, say very little (men love mystique), and wait for the messages to roll in. It's like being the new girl at school, at a time in the school year when the boys have grown tired of the present feminine selection. Respond to the guys you like at least a day later, no matter how much you like him. If he only says *hi, hey, sup or que pasa,* he gets no response. No face-to-face rejection necessary or desired. Based on a picture and a blurb, we get to filter. Sift through the insufferable to reach the tolerable, then search the tolerable to find the exceptions. With online dating, there are very few exceptions. After golf, I feel like Danny Ray may be an exception.

I drive home recalling our conversation at the bar. Atop padded stools, bolted to the floor, Danny Ray brings up race, saying his father died only a few months ago and that, he was an unapologetic racist and bigot. I'm not moved by this confession. This is what I expect of a 75-year-old white man born and raised in Crandall, Texas. The surprise would be if he weren't a racist.

Danny Ray starts at a new sentence, his wrinkled brow is an indication this sentence would be juicy, but he declines. I just listen. He has no idea that I'm happy to be brown, that I'm not bitter and that I don't have an innate problem with whites. He talks from a place that gives me permission to be outraged or offended. I just listen.

Danny tells me about a time his black high school football coach came to dinner at their home and he casually referred to another player on his team as a nigger at the dinner table. The coach, his dad and mom all fell silent. I am less intrigued by people using that word than I am about the fact that the coach was invited there at all. But Danny later explains his dad was trying to get him in the position of quarterback for his senior year and felt the best way to get there was to get chummy with the coach. It didn't work. I feel like a fly on the wall in the home of "Middle American-like" family. *This is better than watching Roseanne,* I think. It's clear that my self-worth is not up for grabs, so permission to divulge this devious morsel of inside information is granted. Human beings crave, empoisoned, unsolicited, uncontaminated inside information; whether we like what we hear or not.

Danny Ray tells his mother he's been chatting with, not me specifically me, but a black woman. That he's going to take her out on a date.

"You're going to hell! It's just wrong to date a black person! I just think everybody should stick to their own kind!" Danny Ray mimics his mother and aunts' sentiments, in his version of a high-pitched female voice. I smirk. I notice what looks to be a Hispanic waitress wince, as she clears his glass and wipes the counter, while overhearing his spirited display. I wonder for half a second if she thinks I'm "cooning".

I take the highway all the way home. The lofty effects of the wine, the pot and Xanax are all vanishing. Both windows on the passenger side are cracked about two inches. No ac, I like the warmth, the bar was cold. The fresh, late night summer breeze whips through the car from front to back. My rules for dating: I never make the first move and they don't mean anything until they ask me to be their girlfriend. Then I decide if I want more. No decisions are made this night. Just golf and conversation.

I reach for my garage door opener, creeping down the alley. It's so quiet. *Would you do him?* I ask myself. I exhale pulling forward into the garage. I am both elated and relieved to be home. My thoughts swoon in a million other directions. I puff, shower, then sleep.

CHAPTER FIVE

The Balcony Club

Picture if you will, all the available men in the world swimming across the ocean. Only the men who make it to shore on their own accord are qualified and ready for a positive, lasting relationship. Men, as far as the eye can see. Clawing, grasping, loving, fighting to meet the love of their lives at the shore. The beach is thick with women. Working, waiting, loving and educating as they anticipate their soul-mates arrival. But these women grow impatient. They see him almost there, almost a man, an accomplished man who swam the entire ocean for them. They no longer wait. The women dive into the ocean of men. Clawing, grasping, loving, fighting, to rescue their man. The woman props the man upon her shoulders. Her impatience carries him to shore. She calls her ego love. He is grateful maybe. Is he self-made? Definitely not. I have been her enough times to know that my number one priority is to wait patiently at the shore.

Dallas is a big city that shuts down at 2am, with a limited number of hotspots in comparison to its size. Greenville and McKinney, Deep Elum, Bishop Arts, high-end restaurants, bars, concerts and museums. Urban suburban. All the same. The day after Top Golf I get a text.

Danny Ray: I had a great time last night.

Me: so did I, thx for dinner

I don't fix my grammar for him.

Tacos for dinner. I stand in the checkout line at the Tom Thumb. One pound of ground beef (grass fed), one large white onion, one green pepper and one taco dinner kit. I whisper my list out loud as Danny's next text comes in.

Danny Ray: r u busy Friday night?

Me: maybe

Danny Ray: live music, dinner and drinks with me?

For me, live music is orgasmic. I want that night, the dinner, the music and the drinks... and it comes with the man. I like Danny Ray. He's cool. No butterflies, but I like that he's showing consistency. He's action centered. He calls just to say good night, I answer *yes* then. We have a short conversation about past jobs where I mention once being a merchandiser for Pepsi and he says he did speed for most of his twenties while on the rodeo circuit here in Texas. He lights up with detail about his glory days. Swinging with his wife and other couples, staying up for days at a time and making tons of money doing menial work for the railroad. Danny misses those days, but his life is better without it. Without speed, which is like meth, he explains, but much milder twenty years ago when he partook, than it is now. He made a decision to quit and never look back. I'm not put off by this. I'm not attached to him or his story. I let him reveal himself to me, no matter what that looks like.

I put chatting with him after quality time with my girls and he explains that he doesn't expect anything else. Danny Ray asks about the girls, not like a pedophile would, but like a person who enjoys family does. He thinks it's funny that I refer to them as the big one and the little one. They are two years apart. One is the smallest kid and one is the biggest. I keep it simple.

Friday night we arrive at *Mi Cocina* in Lakewood. Nice restaurants on Friday nights, in Dallas, are crowded. People pour down the block at some spots in Bishop Arts District, socializing and anticipating a meal with family and friends they've looked forward to all week. Saturday nights are much the same. The waits can be long but are light and easy and expected. There's space to breathe.

When Danny Ray requests a table for two, the server looks past me. Danny Ray points my way and positions himself closer to me. I just stand there like a royal subject, with full expectation that this slight misunderstanding doesn't need me to lift one finger. Although, I do want to help her pick up her cracked face from all over these shiny marble floors, but our table is ready. We are front and center. The energy is refreshing. Lots of happy people. I popped a Xanax and took a puff before I left home. Danny Ray doesn't make me anxious. Anxiety is just my energy's preferred vessel of manifestation.

Anxiety is my default. It's my resting place. I don't struggle with it anymore, it just is. Like sleeping, breathing, thinking.

Danny Ray is so attentive that I almost forget that I'm not in love. He doesn't flirt with me like he wants to. He's afraid to push romance because I'm black, he confessed in our brief phone conversation the night before.

Someday, one day, I want to, when my son is older. Danny goes on about who he is, which for him, boils down to what he does. *Sophisticated procrastination,* I think as he speaks. I'm guilty too, but I'm conscious of it. I wonder as Danny speaks, what Eckhart Tolle would say. I see time as always slipping into the future. Like an hour-glass glued to a table. I give myself and my daughters everything possible, now. They go to ballet now, I have a yoga membership now, I travel the world now. I want to say tomorrow never comes, but it's a cliché that will go under-heard, as great clichés often do.

Tim is Danny's son. He tosses Tim's name into the conversation as if I'm in his movie, and I caught it after the first fifteen minutes had already passed. I silently play catch up. It is my job to *google* my brain for his references. I wait, use context clues and gather that he's talking about his pride and joy, baseball playing, blond hair, blue-eyed son. Danny has him on a pedestal.

I fast forward children when I picture them in my mind. I see them as a full human being, personality overflowing, physical features sealed. I teach baseball players in my Monday and Wednesday morning class. There's six of them in one class. Anglo, mostly six feet or taller, shiny, layered hair and pearly, straight teeth. They all look like somebody's pride and joy, on somebody's pedestal. I see Tim as the older boys I teach but with the spirit of a child. These baseball players question an athletes' need for computer science each class. They are *actually* as privileged in this world as I naturally feel.

I don't look around the busy Mexican bistro to see who's looking at me. I'm with Danny and that's enough. I *know* they're looking. I guess I would too. I order fajitas with steak and shrimp, guacamole, lime and a glass of chardonnay. He orders the same, no shrimp with a Coors light.

We wait and banter like familiar acquaintances. Just present.

"Tim's got a baseball game tomorrow at 9, then I'm going to the gym. After that I guess I'll take a nap, eat, shower...then see what you're up to darling..." Danny Ray smiles in that Podunk way, gulping down his Coors light just before raising one finger to the waitress, waiting for eye contact and then pointing to his near empty glass. Everything is a dance for him, the world is at his feet and he doesn't know anything different.

I sip my wine. I'm in a good mood and I'm not anxious. The Xanax, the pot and the chardonnay are all doing their thing, containing and muffling my edge.

"What you got going tomorrow sweet heart?" Danny Ray pushes his empty away.

"Well..." I take my time, we contrast in that way too.

"If you want, you can bring the girls to Tim's game tomorrow. There's a playground near the field, we can grab food afterwards..." he waits, not for my response but for his next sentence to form and topple out of his mouth. Danny Ray forms sentences, speaks, forms sentences, speaks, asks questions and answers himself. I think when I'm taking care of my daughters, I think around my family, I think at work, I think alone. With Danny Ray, my thinking has no space to consume me. I like not thinking. He creates the next moment without hesitation. Before I have time to think.

Fresh sliced strips of seasoned steak and colorful peppers sizzle on the cast iron as they land on the bright white tablecloths. We clear space for our food like two air traffic controllers holding lighted batons. Everything is perfect.

Danny Ray is a handy man, a hard-worker. His calloused hands reveal this before he does.

"I can do anything around the house. Paint, carpentry, roofing, electrical...you name it...I can help you if you need something." He shoves a spoon full of frijoles into his gullet, some fall back onto his plate, like little paratroopers jumping into rough terrain. He eats fast. He inhales, skips savoring.

"Really...well that's cool..." I wait until my mouth is ninety-five percent empty.

"Yeah...I been doing construction on the side for about twenty years. In one day I make about $200 dollars. And that's just extra." He chuckles at his cleverness in beating the worker bee system.

I don't discuss money. I don't date men who expect me to pay for dates. I see no benefit there. Danny Ray likes discussing money, complaining about it, earning it, finagling it and for now, spending it, on me, an investment.

"I have over $30,000 dollars in Tim's college fund. He doesn't even know it."

"Well...that's good..." I'm riding the coat tails of this conversation as Danny forges on.

The waiter returns, asking if we need more drinks or anything else that might increase his tip. The waiter is flamboyant. He's only a foot or two from the table and Danny Ray gives him a longer glance than he thinks, then assures me, mostly his self, that, *Tim ain't going to be no fairy.* I giggle at the word fairy. I think, *an antiquated slur and mindset to match*. I'm floating more after more wine, but just enough.

We get the check. No to-go boxes. Danny is too in the moment for doggie bags. I like that. We head upstairs to the Balcony Club. The stairs are long and thin. They look steeper than they feel. We walk in, we're noticed. Danny Ray, taller than most, parts the thin, congested walkway, acquiring two lucky seats at the crowded bar. The live band is so loud and delicious. I can hear every cord on the guitar, every octave of the scruffy band leader's voice. I think of an orgasm. When I'm feeling good I always think of orgasms. Then back to Danny. He orders more drinks. By now I know I've had my limit, but I sip just to make sure I don't come down. I'm not ready. I wonder if we are as odd a couple as I feel. I don't like to be analyzed, just being observed is enough, but I do realize, observation and analysis come hand-in-hand for most. For me they are separate.

I don't have cable television at home. Each time the topic comes up, CNN, MSNBC, FOX, HBO, I gently remind Danny Ray that I don't watch. Everyone assumes. Reality TV is the most common assumption of familiarity. I don't know any of those people. And neither does anyone else. It's all smoke and mirrors.

The media climate has become very race conscious. I miss out on all the Ferguson and Baltimore row. But it's in the air. I feel it. The resistance to offend, stir the pot, poke the bear. I don't have an opinion, too many microscopic details that are largely unknown. My 'middle-of-the-roadness is solidified in college. You learn to argue for and against everything. If you go to the right school, you leave knowing that history is always written by the victors, all over the world, since the beginning of the world. I accept this human fate. You also know that everyone assumes they have the only truth in a world of many truths. Human truths are, thick, consuming, exclusive, selfish. Danny seems locked into his 'truths'.

The band plays a mixture of blues and some 50's American Rock and Roll. Songs that have been used since their existence, in commercials, by high school marching bands and for political campaigns.

"Don't stop thinking about tomorrow, don't stop, it'll soon be here..." I tap my feet, smile at Danny Ray who's still trying to figure me out. I sip my wine once more for good measure.

"You know I was watching a comedy show once and the black woman kept saying, you don't touch a black woman's hair..." Danny Ray recounts out of the blue, then holds for a reaction, but tries not to show this. I don't get off on torturing white people with my blackness. I fill the space he leaves.

"Why is that?" I shout over the band, leaning in. I do know this stereotype, but I like pretending I don't.

Danny Ray fumbles. He fumbles more than his usual self because he cares about what I think. His desire to not care also fills the space.

"I don't know...she was just like, you don't touch a black woman's hair..." he hunches, gulps his beer.

"Did she have a weave or a wig?" I still pretend this topic in unfamiliar.

"I have no idea, I just thought it was funny when I saw it..." He raises that index finger for another Coors light. I don't let him off my ride, the *White Guilt Express*.

The White Guilt Express shows up when a white person finds themselves in a conversation with someone of any minority race or ethnicity; and is caught off guard displaying or expressing some belief, value or norm that feeds into a misconception or stereotype about that minority they didn't even know they held. *All Aboard.*

I think, *maybe I do like wielding my blackness,* but only when the red carpet is laid out for me to do so.

"Oh...okay..." I turn back towards the band, Danny changes the subject. I chuckle on the inside. I wonder if most black women would have found offense in that. I tend to be above offense. I only allow passengers on the White Guilt Express if I hope to teach, never to simply taunt, as tempting as that may be.

The band Danny wants to see doesn't arrive for another thirty minutes. The band that is currently rocking the house announces a break. The saxophonist has long mingled steely hair, sort of shallow around the forehead. He's happy with his saxophone. His saxophone is home for him, his sweet spot. The piano player is young, maybe Asian, maybe a rookie. His eyes carefully follow the music propped atop the keyboard. He's the odd ball, visually. The lead singer with the guitar has spunk, fire and grace all at once. Love is in his voice. What a gift. And the middle aged white woman dancing about in front of the small platform, banging her tambourine to every song. Wife? Groupie? Band member? I'm having a great time.

When the live band stops. A stereo continues to play in the background. There is such a difference in the feeling. Empty, light and airy. Stereo music is enough but is not whole.

"Good evening you too...I'm Ernie..." a short and stout older gentleman who had been jigging front and center, with a drink in one hand while the band played, makes his way to us. Danny Ray eagerly replies. He likes people in general.

I tell Ernie my name as I shake his clammy, old hands with the tips of my fingers. My stranger handshake. Danny does the same, with his whole hand instead. Old, white, clammy hands are familiar to him.

"Is this y'alls first time here?" he asks, full of jolliness. This is how he passes his night.

"This is our second date...neither of us ever been here before. We came to see the band that starts at nine and just got here early." Danny answers.

"Oh really, well congrats on the date, you're one lucky fella," he stands between us touching the back of Danny's stool and between the shoulder blades of my back. He gives me the dirty-old-man once over. Ernie grabs a stool and pulls it up next to Danny. He begins with the history of the club. And soon the dirty jokes. I go to the restroom. I know old white men well enough to know that the race jokes could be next.

My hair is in two strand twists. I'm wearing a little flowy sundress, purple with flowers and spaghetti straps. Flat sandals. I check my makeup at the mirror. The backroom of this joint has a 1940's old Hollywood feel. Forty or fifty-year-old gold hued drapes, heavy too, shag carpeting with patterned, antique chairs. I picture Sammy Davis Jr. waiting in this plush foyer, before being called onto the stage. I feel the glamour now removed. I feel the energy of the passion and happenings this dusty foyer held. Its rich. I think, *this is wealth.* I feel it.

This night, I let Danny drive me. He's a good person, seeing this is easy. I listen to my intuition and let my guard down. He's had three beers in two hours. This time I count. While the band takes five, we retreat to the outdoor patio. It's chilly in the club. The balmy summer air feels like relief. Our juxtaposition is leading the way.

"Bitch..." Danny Ray mumbles below his breath. Before I could muster up some sort of reaction, I watch his eyes follow the lady behind me. She's tall, a redhead, big hair, big aura. She's smoking her cigarette the way women of her age do, who smoke Virginia Slims. She's carefree, blowing her smoke directly into the back of my space. Danny is visibly annoyed. I point at the sign that designates this spot as a smoking zone. Danny rolls his eyes. "I don't care!" he spouts. "It's called respect." He grunts.

I chuckle.

We make our way back into the bar, which is now overrun with a younger crowd as nine o'clock approaches. The sea of baby boomers skedaddle. I'm intrigued by the seamless transition from old to young. Sophisticated young, but all young nonetheless.

Danny and I steal a booth during this transition. It's right in front of the band and has cushioned seats. I sit, then Danny.

"You want more wine darling?"

"No thanks..." my stomach gurgled at the thought of being hungover. I'm still floating. Not as high. But enough.

"You should have brought your pot with you, you could have smoked it in the car. Jazz is better when you're high. Back when I could smoke I use to do it all day, from morning to night." Danny is thoroughly pleased that I smoke pot. It opens some portal for him. Boundless, colorless, judgeless. He stays away from any substance that might cost him his job or the life he's built. For now, Danny is content living vicariously through me.

I usually don't discuss pot, but I humor him.

"My weed never leaves the house." I sip the water the waitress brought only a few seconds earlier, holding the straw with my pinky extended.

"Why not? You keep hanging with me and we're gonna break some of those rules?" *Podunk grin*

This Magnolia chick, who sings lead in the band is a diva akin to Jill Scott, Angie Stone or Ledisi. She's bad. She doesn't introduce herself. She lets her vocals speak for her. Now *this* band is funk personified. Freedom personified. The base player is wearing an old-school fedora, with a blue pinstripe trailing the edges of his brim. He doesn't remove his shades. This saxophonist is grooving, as if he's hearing the music for the first time tonight. The music is a part of his muscle memory. He can't explain it. The drummer is carefree, brown and happy. They even have a trumpeter. They're so New Orleans.

Magnolia begins her seductive performance with Jill Scott's Long Walk. This song I've heard at least a thousand times. She made it brand new.

Danny Ray watches me mouth the words to a song he's never heard. He taps his feet to this beat. I feel at home now, from observed to observer.

Magnolia sings neo-soul hit after neo-soul hit. This is black music in a white space. I think of an orgasm.

Before last call we head home. That's four and a half Coors lights in four hours. I figure we'd live. Danny's posture is still proper. He opens every door without fail, and I let him. I have a public handle phobia. I prefer not to touch them, any kind. Door handles, gas pumps, stair railings, the little latch on bathroom stalls. This is me.

We arrive to the curb adjacent to my quaint, suburban home. Even silence has gone to sleep, its dead. Danny Ray escorts me up the walkway. I position my body and face towards the door. I jiggle the keys around, working with very little light to find the hole. Danny Ray is right behind me. I sense his anticipation. The moment is moving fast. Too fast for me to think. I have no memory of this moment. It unfolds brand new, as do most moments that are uncalculated and unrehearsed. I have nothing inside of me to manufacture. It's like I hover and watch myself at the door. Like a television drama, I wait for what's next. Uncontrived, I just wait. I open the door and place my right foot in. I turn half way towards Danny.

"Well good night, I had a good time." I grin. Excluding my physical body, all parts of me are already indoors, in pajamas, puffing, and letting a movie watch me. *I just have to get through the next minute or two,* I think.

"My pleasure darling." He steps back, realizing tonight will not be a first kiss night.

"Well, I'll be out of town for work this week, but I'd love to get together again." Just like a movie, Danny is a true suitor. I try not to compare him to other guys, but humans only have previously collected data to work with.

"Sure. Good night" My first inclination is to shake his hand, so I do. I have a week to decide if I'm going to see him again. I exhale. I feel free. Back to thinking and watching my thoughts. Round and round. I drift off to sleep thinking about how incredibly white Danny is.

JAMEELAH RAOOF

CHAPTER SIX

Lonny's Truck

Danny works as some sort of supervisor for the railroad. They mostly travel around East and West Texas, but his current position keeps him home more often, which he says is best for he and Tim's relationship. As often as he mentions his son, Danny mentions his ex. They are one entity in his mind, even if he doesn't see it that way.

I read his online profile thoroughly. I know Danny is not divorced yet. He has confirmed this fact several times in casual conversation. One evening online, I check the Kaufman County public records to verify that he has filed and is not potentially dragging me into a sullen environment. According to county records, a petition for divorce was filed by her a year earlier and is pending. I exonerate him, for now.

"Hello, I'm back...that was Danielle picking up Tim." He puts me on hold while he sees Tim off.

"No problem." I reply.

"I don't want you to think that me and my ex are together in any way what so ever..." Danny's high-pitched Texas twang rings higher. "I mean there is no possibility at all!" He continues. "She's a pretty good mom, but she's nuts. And I know you haven't seen her but she's huge. Every year she gets bigger and bigger. I'm worried it may start to embarrass Tim." Danny holds back nothing.

At my job, I work with all these old stuffy types. They have no idea how old and how white they are. Sitting in meetings is like watching a game of Snakes and Ladders they all go through an exorbitant amount of trouble just to say exactly what's on their minds. They are so congested, living small, looking big. Each catering to one another's emotional maladies. Danny Ray is the polar opposite of them.

"I just want to make sure you know that that piece of paper means nothing." Danny Ray explains, still utilizing the full version of his high-pitched twang. He explains some more. He becomes inaudible, to me. Like Jeff Boomhauer. On my end, I sit back on my bed, with my legs straight, ankles crossed. I take a puff, listen, navigate Netflix, sip my sweet tea, take a puff and listen.

He halts. I use my mental rewind button to scan my thoughts. *Did he ask me something?* I pause, trying to avoid him noticing my lack of investment in what he's saying.

"I understand, we're just getting to know each other." Danny adds. His chuckle trails off. My words are as loose as I am. I attempt to validate the conversation with a couple of mm-hmms, but I'm sleepy.

"See I like you...we can talk to each other, communicate like adults...that's important to me in what I'm looking for in a mate..." Danny adds.

"Yep...always good to know what you want..." I reply.

"So, what you got going tomorrow sweetheart?" His sharp twang relaxes.

My daughters are with their dad on Wednesday evenings until Thursday afternoons. I told Danny this the day we met.

Tomorrow hasn't occurred to me yet. I don't plan my Wednesday nights.

"Early yoga, grading at home, grab something to eat..." I trail off.

"Well I'm off tomorrow so you wanna get food with me around noon, then find something else to do? I'll plan something else for us to do don't worry." Danny adds with eagerness. I feel pushed. I enjoy my free time. I'm reluctant to give it away so far in advance.

"Sounds good." I hesitate, but Danny doesn't read into it. He doesn't read into anything. He only tunes into having his expectations met.

"Alright sweetheart. Do you want me to just come or do I need to call first?"

"Calling is good."

"Good night darling."

"Good night."

I change our date to six in the evening.

Danny Ray rings the doorbell. I open the door just wide enough for him to see the foyer. I step out.

"Well you look beautiful...Hell, you always look good. I don't think there's a thing you can wear that you wouldn't look beautiful in..." Podunk grin. I want to hand him a piece of straw.

I wear some Aztec printed skinny jeans, a lacy, buttery yellow top and my red hair, fluffy, curly, out and free. Gladiator flats for comfort.

Danny Ray opens the passenger side of a little black Toyota, or Honda or Hyundai, I don't check.

"Have you been drinking...am I safe?" I chuckle nervously, strapping my seatbelt on. Danny seems extra loose.

"Baby I'm the safest guy you gone ever meet. I'm gone get you back home in one piece." He smashes the accelerator.

We stop at the red light. The sun is setting. Danny pulls off his shades. He let his buzz cut grow out and now the sides are faded and short. Now I'm thinking Hawk from The Avengers. His skin looks leathery, maybe tanned. He has country western music playing.

He sings along.

If you want to impress me baby here's my plan,

All you got to do is put a drink in my hand...

Fill it up or throw it down,

When you drive me home, take the long way around,

You be my Lois Lane, I'll be your Super Man,

All you got to do is put a drink in my hand...

We hop off interstate 635 somewhere around Mesquite. We pull into an apartment complex. Not precisely poor but the working-class and their families. The proletariat, mostly white. Danny says we're going to a drive-in movie theater, so he needs to grab his roommate's pickup. He brings blankets and chairs, so we can sit in the bed of the truck to watch the movie. I'm intrigued.

We park, Danny hops out and heads up the stairs on the far-right end of the building. Almost instantly, he comes back down with a brunette, very pale, forties, worker bee, plain. We wait about five minutes before Lonny pulls into the parking lot in his large black pick-up truck. He parks in a hurry. Danny comes back to the car, opening the passenger side front door.

Lonny is average height, round, middle aged with a face of a 35-year-old. White guy. Mostly bald. He lives in Danny's guest bedroom. Danny tells me how Lonny pays him $600 a month and how he's doing Lonny a favor because his request is a bargain. And Lonny pays the cable bill too.

"Come on sweet heart." Danny waits for me to exit. I have a Xanax sitting on my tongue. I swallow it before I place my feet on the ground.

I stand there with my purse as Lonny vigorously removes every trace of his daily life from the cab of his truck. He smiles, using the back of his hand to wipe the beads of sweat off his forehead.

Danny, with his arms folded, makes small talk with Lonny's girlfriend, the plain brunette. "So, where you work?"

She responds taking her time. "In Addison...yep...I take the toll way straight there."

Danny nods his head, partially watching Lonny from the corner of his eye.

"Oh, this is my date Yasminah...she's a college professor." She doesn't look at me for a few seconds. I feel awkward. Then, "Hi, I'm Lisa." Her arms are folded too. I mirror her smile. She looks at me briefly. Lisa has two teenage daughters living in her apartment with her. They come down to the parking lot, snickering with each other, watching the adults closely.

"Get your ass over there and help Lonny clean out that truck." Danny spouted at Lisa, sealing his playful demand with a, "Ha!"

Lisa doesn't smile. She walks over to Lonny. "He doesn't get to talk to me like that...you need to tell him something." Lonny is still shuffling around. Moving things. A plastic bag in one hand a rag to wipe in the other. I notice myself, analyzing their dynamic. "Did you hear me...he doesn't get to talk to me like that! I told you that before!" She grows a bit louder, a bit more serious.

Lonny wipes a few more beads of sweat from his forehead with the back of his hand. "Okay...okay...I heard you...Geesh!" He hushes his tone and her with a gutless quality about himself. Lonny glances up to see if I'm watching. "Hi, I'm Lonny." He reaches out to shake my hand through the open doors of the vehicle. I lean through, his hands are clammy. He smiles and wipes his forehead once more.

Danny receives a call. "Who's this?" He's short. Two seconds later. "Nope, no can do...on a date!" He ends the call and helps me hop into the front seat of the pick-up. The same person calls again. "Shit!" Danny answers. "I'm on a date!" He shouts and ends the call once again. I think for a moment, *where the hell am I, who are these people and why am I here?* This feels below my pay grade, and so culturally foreign.

Lisa steps back near her daughters, he eyes scan me from my bright red hair to my hot pink toenails just before they head back up the stairs. Lonny waddles towards the little black car we came in and Danny and I are off.

"Damn, Danielle's trying to get me to watch Tim tonight. I already told her I had a date." He exhales sharply. Pats me on my knee, flashes his grin as if it's a reset button.

We stop at the gas station. Danny puts ten dollars' worth of gas into Lonny's truck. He goes into the service station and comes out with a small bag of assorted candies.

"If you buy it here its three dollars...but if you buy it at the theater, it's three times that amount." He puffs his chest, beating the system once more. I take the candy and I'm grateful for it.

Danny spills some of his Monster energy drink onto the front seat. "Fuck it...it ain't mine." He mumbles, referring to Lonny's truck.

"You okay darling?" Danny asks. "Its hot as shit out there!" He adds.

"Perfect." I chew on my candy, cherry sours and lemonheads.

I've never been to a drive-in theater before. This one is thirty miles down the highway in a small, out-of-the-way town named Ennis. The sun is nearly set when we arrive to the large dessert-like field sprinkled with gigantic movie screens. They are huge and each facing a large field with old fashioned posts where the individual car would attach to a wired speaker. But now we use the car radio. This is something different. I'm refreshed.

Families are camped out, kids in pajamas and heaps of them playing in the beds of trucks. Trucks decorated with both American and Confederate flags. They look happy. Hundreds of people. This is a white space, once again I feel like a spectator.

Its seventy-five degrees, a Fall seventy-five degrees. Still chilly to me, too chilly to sit in the bed of the truck. Danny seems disappointed about my change of heart. I pretend not to notice.

"How long has Lonny and Lisa been dating?" I ask, digging through my bag for a piece of chewing gum.

"A few months. Believe me, they won't be together too much longer. Any woman that stays with Lonny for too long, I know has a few screws loose." He reaches into the spacious back seat for a Coors light, from a half empty case he discreetly brought along. He cracks the top. Licks the rising foam. "You want one dear?"

"No, I'm okay." I puffed before leaving home. The Xanax is kicking in. I'm relaxed.

"What's wrong with Lonny?"

"He's a piece of shit. Lies about everything. Can't trust him." Danny says these words as if they are rehearsed and fit Lonny without question.

"Well, why keep him around?" I find my gum.

"He pays his rent." Danny is quick.

I gaze straight ahead at the big white screen. I notice moving figures starting to show. It's almost dark enough.

We finish one romantic comedy and move on to the next, blaze through an entire large popcorn and both boxes of candy. The more beer Danny drinks, the more he talks. He's working on his fourth beer in three hours. I just listen. We're not touching the whole time we watch the movies. The cab is so large, there's no expectation to do so. With only thirty minutes left before the last movie is over, we're both on the edge of falling asleep. We're about forty-five minutes to an hour from my home. All I can think about is wanting my bed.

We ride to my house in near silence. Good, comfortable silence.

Danny jumps out. I wait for him to open my door. I hold one of his hands as if I'm stepping off a carriage, or a docked boat. I get to my door, same routine as last time. He doesn't push for affection.

"Good night sweetheart...I had a great time." His voice, mostly base-filled and tired. No twang.

I give him a quick hug. "Thanks for the date. I had a great time too." We part. The more time I spend with Danny, the more his raw approach to life is exposed. He is not calculated like me, nor does he consider not fitting in anywhere he goes. Before I go to bed this night, I drift off trying to comprehend his world, how he interacts on a symbolic level and how his world perceives him.

Freedom to just be is all he knows, I feel fearless in his world simply because he is.

CHAPTER

SEVEN

Dinner in Crandall

This semester I'm teaching mostly introductory courses. Which means I don't have to study alongside my students. In these classes, I'm omniscient. I float from one topic to the next. Motherboards, networks, social media, smart phones, processors, operating systems. Iphones, Ipads, Itunes...I not interested, I often say, and the students laugh.

I use that joke every semester. I don't mind seeming old to them.

My phone vibrates below the podium in my nine am class. I keep lecturing. It vibrates again, and again and once again. I separate the students into independent learning groups. They ask questions, but I'm anxious and I want to check my phone. I'm not as extroverted as I appear to be in front of the class. I want them to release me to my solitude and focus on themselves for a while. I'm a performer, in and out, close the curtains, exit the building through the back door.

They are engaging in their group assignment as I bounce around the room. Time flies by. "Any questions?" I ask while scanning the room from right to left. No hands are raised.

"Ya'll are good, see you next week." I exhale, grab my things and make a beeline for my office. I'm bursting with anticipation, each step I get closer to dropping the arm full of supplies I carry and reading the messages. My secrets. Which all come from a familiar number, I've yet to save into my phone.

9:36 am: Morning darling.

9:38 am: I had a great time with you last night.

9:42 am: You looked beautiful

9:45 am: Too bad it had to end.

9:55 am: You ignoring me??

10:01 am: Joking...

I smile. Not smitten, amused. Danny is persistent. I respect persistence. I only reply to his messages once.

10:55 am: Good morning silly.

Yoga at noon. Shower, eat, pick up my babies. Homework, playtime, baths, dinner, story, bedtime. Mommy puffs, then sleeps. Six am, it starts again. Like a sun salutation in yoga, I pass through this routine daily. At the pace of my own breath. Nothing from Danny this day, I don't flinch but I do wonder.

Three more days of my routine pass and Danny calls. I miss his calls twice that day. He texts near bedtime.

Danny: You mind if I cook for you this weekend?

Me: So, you want me to come to your house?

Danny: Is that a bad idea?

Me: You might be crazy... I chuckle to myself.

Danny: I am, but you'll still be alright...

Me: I'm a parent!

Danny: So am I... you might be the dangerous one...

Me: Touche...

Danny: I can cook. I can make this chicken breast dish I make and some veggies. Just think about it...

Me: (30 minutes later) What time?

Later that night I watch a program about racism in America. Blacks are poor, whites are evil and no bright light at the end of that tunnel. I'm drawn to interracial couples on social media. How do they connect internally, externally? I read comments on their pictures. Black woman, white man is less common but more popular. More forgiven. She takes control of her love life, she doesn't wait for the black man that has publicly, historically discarded her. She creates happiness. She takes an alternate route.

Dinner. I arrive ten minutes after the time I say I will. He lives forty highway minutes away. Before leaving home, I search Danny's address. Check out a street view. It's clean, suburban, near a baseball field, a bit country. Small house, Zillow says 1,504 square feet.

There's an in-ground pool in the back yard, it's on a corner lot.

As I drive into his town it's getting dark, burnt orange, magenta, plum then navy skies. I creep into the driveway. My tires make that gravely sound. I'm frozen with unfamiliarity. The house looks just like the street view. I see two dogs run around from behind the house and right up to the fence. A chain-linked fence, rusted, warped and familiar, like in movies. They bark for attention. I pop two Xanax tonight. Tonight, this night, I'm nervous. *Should I just leave?,* I think. I sit in my car absorbing the present moment.

My breath is shallow, stomach clinched. *Why am I here? Do I even know this guy?* The screen door slams like the old southern kind. The kind made of wood and metal screen. Danny's tall, muscular silhouette stood at my car door. He looks like a cowboy, slight bow legs and all. Like Walt Longmire, warm and trustworthy, but mightily flawed. He seems different tonight. The street light behind him doesn't allow me to see his face clearly. I smile anyway. We exchange a quick hug before walking into his home. I set one foot in, scan the place, and think, *he's country.* I smell chicken, puppies, bleach, and fabric softener.

He babbles, I'm spaced-out. I listen well when I'm spaced-out. From the couch, I eyeball an off-brand potato chip bag nailed to the kitchen wall. Danny explains to me that he had a deaf blue heeler, who used to run all around the neighborhood and one day finds a bag of half eaten potato chips on the ground, near the ball park. He goes into the bag nose first. The bag gets stuck. The blue heeler stumbles into the street, unable to hear and because of the chip bag, unable to see. He's run over and dies. Danny nails the bag from said incident to his kitchen wall.

Fifteen hundred square feet sounds a lot smaller than it actually feels. Although, from the driveway, I could watch his television. It's at least sixty inches diagonally, and the main attraction in his home. Danny has a dusky brown leather recliner and an equally dusky brown leather sectional. Next to the kitchen there are two large slide doors that lead to the back yard. The neglected pool has no water in it. The house is clean enough, so I decide that It's comfortable.

I see a gun on the shelf above the kitchen counter, where the gnats that trickle in from outside swarm near the light.

"Is that a weapon?" My shoulders lift a little. I vacillate between an out of body experience and a very in body one.

Danny glances back. His eyes search for the object I'm referring to. He laughs.

"It's a bb gun." He grabs it from the high shelf, slides open the back door, points the bb gun toward his back fence and pulls the trigger, three to four times in a row. With every pop I flinch as an experience that is different unfolds moment by moment. Three to four small clacks. Like highway pebbles flung at a windshield. He hands it to me. I point and pull the trigger once. I don't like how it feels. *Guns kill*, rattles around in my thoughts, just a flash. Danny laughs deeper, whispering the word weapon to himself. Subconsciously we explore the mixing of our space. We secretly gauge it.

One dining table, two chairs, light brown wood laminate flooring with slight moisture damage near the seams. The base molding has been removed. The walls are painted neutral colors. Many unfinished projects, from missing cabinet knobs to a fridge that sounds as if it is struggling to cool. There is no feminine energy in Danny's space.

"Is Lonny not here? I see his truck." I sit onto the sectional with the glass of wine Danny placed into my hand a few seconds earlier, when he giggled about me saying the word weapon.

"He ain't here. That little black car we rode in is his too. My Volkswagen is in the shop and my Saturn is outside. It's a piece of shit. The Bronco needs a battery. I wouldn't ride you in any of those cars. I just use Lonny's, hell he don't give a damn." Danny's checking on the glass pan in the oven that contains our main dish. He has on a baby blue tank and basketball shorts. Barefoot. "You're gonna love my Volkswagen...just wait..."

Danny serves dinner. Two Styrofoam plates, mixed veggies, chicken in a red sauce, topped with cheese. It's edible. We discuss his exes.

"We were just a bad combination." Danny says of his ex-girlfriend, not his soon to be ex-wife. "She liked to drink too much and so did I, with her...anyway," he glances up to witness my reaction. The chicken is tender. Not too much cheese, the veggies are unseasoned. The stereotype of white people not seasoning their food flash in my head.

"I got you something for dessert." Danny smiles. I'm hoping cheesecake. He returns with a joint.

He hands it to me. "You won't believe who brought that over..." I wait. "My ex, Tim's mom. I told her I had a date tonight and that you smoke pot and she said I'll bring some over." He hunches his shoulders. I'm intrigued by their dynamic.

"Oh...well that's nice..." I check in to see if I feel any kind of certain way. I don't.

We head outside, pass the waterless pool, a waterless hot tub and then stroll into a large metal shed. Like the kind mechanic shops use to move motors and transmissions around. The kind where medium-sized drug deals go down on television dramas.

"Grrrrr....grrrrr..." Danny's dog growls at me. Just one of them. They appear out of the darkness. They rattle the uncontained foliage in the back yard. I almost bend the joint. Dogs make me anxious. They're mid-sized dogs, both blue heelers. The silent one, Danny informs me is deaf like the one that died.

"Get on over here!" He bends forward towards the dogs, scratching and rubbing them under their chins and around their ears. Both are girls. Shark and Heaven. Shark is the white one, the younger one, the deaf one. Heaven is old and territorial. Danny throws a stick over their heads and into the darkness, neither dog fetches. They hang out, observing us. The large shed is well lit. The inside is just as imagined. Tools, car parts, pool table, rusted stools, all sorts of manly equipment. Danny shows me his 1980s stereo with bulbs of some sort. He blasts a bluesy tune loud enough to make the dogs walk away. Once he feels his demonstration of his stereo receiver is sufficient he lowers the volume and moves on.

"The boys don't even use it anymore." He points across the pitch-black yard in the direction of a large, well-made treehouse, complete with a zip line. One of the only finished projects on his property.

"Boys?" I respond, remembering that we've only discussed one son.

"Oh yeah...I have another son. Well he's not really my son. It's my cousin's boy. He's my black son." Danny bursts into his high-pitched laugh. I nod and grin. Awaiting the automatic explanation that generally follows a revelation of this intrigue. "His dad's black." He scrambles for his phone to show me a picture of his biological son Tim and his little cousin. They are the same age and practically the same color. I smile at the boys. Danny watches my face. "His dad's creole." Danny adds. I ponder for a moment about how blackness is so significant to white people. Black first then everything else.

"Yes...I can see that." I reply. I can see the African in the boy's features. Danny looks at me as if the boy's blackness should mean something significant to me. I'm not sure why but the boy's black DNA is important to him. He seems proud, but maybe for the wrong reasons. Like this gives him some level of street cred (which I'm sure I would never be street enough to bestow upon him) or the inside track to understanding whatever it is Danny perceives black to mean, both consciously and subconsciously. Like when an old professor of mine, kept going on about discovering black DNA in his genealogy report. He kept looking my way, me being the only black person that white space. I remember the professor's confession making me feel uncomfortable, like my blackness was a novelty item to him. I haven't decided if feel this way with Danny.

"My cousin only dates black men. And I don't mean to sound rude, but she picks the most piece of shit black men she can find." His face recoils in disbelief. I wonder why Danny feels the quality of his cousin's black boyfriends should affect me, why should I feel slighted by his disgust with the bad behavior of this one black man?

"She picks the wrong men who happen to be black." I slide this comment into the open space.

"Well yeah...it's not a real factor, it's just a fact about the men my cousin picks..." He turns away, moving towards the corner of the garage where some large discarded items reside.

"This here is a swing that used to hang on the front porch." Danny points at a large wooden swing with two heavy chains attached to it.

"Danielle, my ex, always thinks that I'm out to get her. When we first split up, and she moved out. She took the Volkswagen that I told you is in the shop...?" I nod. "She pulled down the swing, got pissed off 'cause I wouldn't help her, threw it on top of the car and drove down the street with it until it fell off at the corner..." Danny looks at me, as if he wonders if he's saying too much. He sighs, then steps back towards the pool table.

"You wanna shoot some pool?" Danny asks, racking the balls with one hand and holding a pool stick in the other. I grew up with a pool table at home. I secretly love beating my dates at pool. I never tell them how good I am before we play. I feel like I'm in a high school boyfriends bedroom and he's showing me all the cool things he's collected in an attempt to impress me.

Before Danny breaks the balls, he walks over with a lighter. I hold up the joint in one hand and create a windproof cave with my other hand. I puff, deep and long. I think, *It's so nice to have pot in this moment.* Danny grabs it as I exhale, hitting it once.

"I thought you couldn't smoke because of your job?" I ask.

"That one little hit ain't gonna make a bit of difference sweetheart. I'm off for the next seven days...besides, I ain't had none in ten years. Darling I'm already high." He grabs his beer, cranks up the stereo, then obliterates the tight triangle of balls. He seems young tonight.

This night we flirt. Danny, barefoot, stands next to me, giving me pointers, as most men do. He leans forward. His arms are peach and muscular. I'm wondering if he tans. He stands up straight again. He's tall. I look straight up towards his face. I try to picture myself kissing him. *What would it be like?* Danny continues to ramble and I just nod. This space reminds me of my childhood home.

This is our fourth date. I try to label this transaction, put bookends on it. *Does he want something? Besides my cookies of course.* While this connection is intriguing. Each time we part ways I don't expect him to call. Part of me doesn't want him to pursue.

We listen to the music. Banter about everything. We continue our new-found comradery into the night and back into the house. The stars are extra bright here. I'm not wearing my spectacles and I see both big and little dippers. We pass the waterless pool once again. This time I point.

"Oh yeah...I had to let the water out to fix the lining around the top edge...I'm a fix it this summer...we use to have all kinds of parties back here. The pool is only four feet deep all the way across." He walks over to the hot tub. "I need a new motor for this one. So much shit to do, and all of it costs money." Danny gripes for a brief spell.

"I just got rid of a hot tub. It was taking up too much space." I add, but he's already moved on.

Danny is walking like the ground is hot coals on his bare feet. He doesn't close the slide door, so the dogs can come and go. Both dogs are relaxing on the floor, in front of the sectional. We sit, in what feels to be the Heaven and Shark's space.

Danny is less chatty since the pot. We decide to watch a movie. I feel him moving closer to me. Each time he moves, he brushes his arm against mine or relaxes his leg right near mine. The sofa is hard. I shuffle around to let the blood in my ass circulate.

"You comfortable sweetheart?" With this question he propels his arm around my shoulders. I lean into him but I'm not relaxed. In seconds I wiggle my way out. I use the ubiquitous task of checking my phone as an excuse to get free.

"I am." I wiggle some more.

"This side of the sectional might not be too soft. I had to put a piece of plywood underneath, so it wouldn't fall through...we can sit on the other side if you want?" He's ready to move at my request.

"No...I'm okay." I'm polite.

Danny takes my hand and rests it in the palm of his. His hands are large. He runs his finger tip along the edges of my hand. It tickles and I giggle.

"I thought you said you didn't wear jeans?" He whispered, running his fingers against the rough texture of my jeans. I can feel myself getting wet. *You're not having sex.* I think to myself. *It's not even an option.*

I turn my face towards his. I know how bad he wants me. His desire is a major source of my confidence in this moment. The light is shadowy.

"I have a couple of pairs..." I swallow. Before I breathe back out, Danny grabs my face firmly with one hand, his pinky finger right below my chin. He presses his lips up against mine. Through the pressure slips his tongue pass my lips like a penis would do a vagina. I'm getting moist. I feel butterflies. A whole field of them. Fluttering, dancing, mesmerizing but I want out. I'm not comfortable in this space, not with him.

He whispers, "You don't know how long I been waiting to kiss you." His index finger passes over my lips as if they are priceless jewels that need only the glance of a superbly trained eye to solidify its value. My lips mesmerize without effort. They are full, supple and curvaceous, his are tight and thin, barely there.

I pull back. Exhale. "I think it's time for me to go." I pull my things together. I'm not sure how I feel.

"You sure about that darling?"

"Huh?" I reply in a mental fog scrambling around.

"You sure you want to leave?" Danny looks confused.

I stand, putting my purse on my shoulder. "Yes...I had fun as usual."

He walks me to my car. Gives me peck on the cheek and tells me to text him once I make it home.

I don't.

CHAPTER EIGHT

The Fall

This entire week, I second guess my choice to not text Danny. I'm not upset if he moves on, but I'm still curious. I stand in front of my kitchen sink, drying dishes and putting them away. The girls demolish their playroom in the background, just before bedtime. I try to understand why I feel attraction for this man. He is so different. Not his skin color, but his whiteness. I'm no stranger to white guys, even if I never considered them a viable long-term candidate, but usually the ones who like me are familiar with blackness. Danny is not. I think, standing here, *I'm better off anyway.*

For six months out of the year I'm a dance mom. Both my girls enjoy ballet lessons, costumes, recitals, the whole gamut. If there is no afterschool ballet then there is the library, reading club, church with grandparents or an afterschool fitness club. Lazy is not an option. Both are in gifted classes and on the A honor roll at their small, exclusive, yet diverse charter school. I am content with my routine. I am happy with my daughters. We live a full life and I am always grateful.

My use of online dating sites only surface out of fear. Fear of being a shut in. Fear of not showing my daughters a quality relationship with a man. And fear of missing my chance to find true love. When Danny doesn't call or text me for the whole week.

Contrary to the way I feel, I don't head back to the dating site to scrounge up the first man my profile attracts. Instead, I delete my account. I resist the urge to fill this space. And resist the urge to judge me and Danny's interactions just yet. I sit in this space, I take no action, just sit.

I do, however, question his motives and I am happy we haven't had sex. Lately I've been reading several books about taking relationships slowly. I use this advice. *If they can't wait, they aren't for you, if they're for you, waiting won't matter.* This is the overall theme of many books on the topic. This trope is a contradiction to every pop culture magazine on the topic, but I choose power. The power to keep my cookies in the jar. It's my choice this time.

A watched phone never rings, is a fitting cliché, and insanely profound. Five days of no calls or texts, I began to let it go. I give myself closure. I don't wait another minute.

Day six. The phone rings. A number I don't recognize pops onto the screen. I'm at my sister's quaint suburban home, where she resides as a single mother of two teenage daughters. I don't visit as much as I use to but instead of sitting alone, creating an unhealthy and unhappy story about Danny, I visit someone. A much needed distraction.

I don't answer the first call. I wait for a message. I don't like taking surprise phone calls. I need a moment to process whether or not I want to talk. That goes for people I know too. Just as the little voicemail symbol shows up on my phone, it rings again. This time its Danny's number. I'm shocked, anxious and curious. I'm open but not too open. I answer.

"Hello..." In my sexy, professional, no-nonsense tone. My ego whispers, *they all come back.*

"Hello...is this Yas...mi...nah?" A burly familiar voice butchers my name. I can't place it, but it's not Danny.

"This is Yasminah." I clear my throat and step into my sister's kitchen. This call feels different. I have emptied myself of all deadly possibilities that explain Danny's silence. He committed suicide. He's in jail. A bad car accident. His ex-shot him. These excuses are distractions. He just doesn't want to call. This is my conclusion. Men make time for women they like.

"Hey, this is Lonny, Danny's friend..." He pauses.

"Yes..." I respond, lost in the unfamiliarity of the moment.

"Danny's been in an accident." He pauses.

"Really?" My heart drops into the pit of my stomach. I think he must be dead. Anxiety floods every inch of my being. I'm not 'in love'

127

but I see that I indeed have love for this person.

"Yep...it's pretty bad too...they're saying he might not make it." Lonny adds to the conversation, simultaneously adding to my panic.

In a matter of seconds my mind is bombarded with question after question. *What kind of accident? Why is he calling me? What am I supposed to learn from this? When did this happen? Is this a trick to get me to not be bothered by his brief disappearance?* I'm confused and flustered. There is no linear processing happening, I am bouncing from one end of space and time to the other end.

"What kind of accident was it?" My throat is dry. I ask a necessary question that I don't truly want the answer to. Lonny sits patiently on the other end.

"He fell off a 30-foot metal building doing some construction work on the side...directly onto the pavement..."

I gasp, having the good fortune of never experiencing such a gruesome accident among my friends and family. With no past experience to draw upon I ask more questions.

"Oh my God...when did this happen?" I reply, almost whispering.

Today is Tuesday. I last spoke to Danny Sunday the week prior, eight days earlier. *Was he in the process of a disappearing act before he hurt himself?* Possibly. *How would Lonny Know?*

"Yesterday Morning..." Lonny replied.

I think, *now what? I'm sorry to hear that, send his family my prayers? Or, where is he being hospitalized and when can I visit?* I take the lead of the Good Samaritan I've seen many times over on television, movies and read about in books. I, with many reservations, rise to the occasion.

Before I could fill silence, Lonny chimed back in.

"He was doing some work on top of the metal building and slipped on a sheet of tin... they say he wasn't wearing his harness..." Lonny speaks as if he's on the six o'clock news. With the depth of his southern drawl, a YouTube video of his testimony would likely go viral. Even remixed.

I swallow. "What hospital is he in? Does he want visitors?"

"He ain't awake honey...he's in a coma...like I said it's pretty bad..." Lonny adds. I push my breath in, then out.

"Well, should I visit him now?" I'm jittery on the inside. I care but Danny's condition isn't tangible yet.

"I'm going to text you his mom's number and the room number...he's at Baylor..." Lonny offers.

"That's fine..." I reply. A few moments of silence pass.

"So where do you work?" Lonny asks. My brain tries to switch gears.

"Me...?" My brows furrow. I think the conversation should be over.

"Yeah..." Lonny replied, with a tone that still does not match the weight of Danny's accident. I could decide that white people just aren't too emotional, or I could decide men aren't. I choose neither.

"I Teach..."

"My girlfriend...Lisa...the one you met. Her oldest just got accepted into SMU...yep."

"Well that's cool. Well, just let me know about Danny. I'll be looking forward to that text." A part of me hopes the text never comes.

"Alright...hopefully he wakes up soon. I was up there today. He's in ICU." Lonny adds as if I'm not in the process of ending our exchange. I say okay and disconnect.

I stand there in my sister's dark kitchen. I'm perplexed. *What do I do here? We haven't had sex or made any commitments. What's the protocol?* Danny has been on this Earth for nearly forty years and I know him for two short weeks and four well-behaved dates. I breathe in deeply, letting the oxygen flow into all of my uncomfortable places.

I don't regret closing my online dating account. Online daters are often too needy. They mostly have a long list of demands for their special someone and rant on about what they're not willing to put up with.

Thirty-nine years old, 6'1", Athletic, blond hair, blue eyes, non-religious, nonsmoker, likes country music, likes to go back-roading, etc. etc. etc.

This is all I really know about Danny. This and four dates of well-behaved moments. I go home this night and Facebook him. I plug in his first and last names, his city too. I recognize the picture immediately. It's one of the four he has displayed in his online dating profile. The one where he says he's looking for a long-term relationship and that he likes to go to the local bar, but doesn't make a habit of it.

His profile picture is the one where he has on no shirt, white linen shorts, standing on the beach, six pack pronounced and eyes squinting from the sun. He looks hot and hot. He has over nine hundred friends. The vast majority from Crandall High school. I flip through his pictures. I put down one album and pick up another. Social media is an ongoing, zero-effort, open invite into a person's life. I see pictures of Danny guzzling beer from a large plastic tube. Another picture of him in a wig and a couple of vulgar talking animal memes peppered throughout.

A picture in his timeline with both his son and the other kid he calls his black son is liked by Danielle Austin, the ex, but still legal wife. I click on her name. Facebook is a rabbit hole of clickable, bits of instant gratification. She uses Facebook often. Most of her profile pictures are face shots. My brain pictures a larger woman as her complete package is slowly revealed twenty or so pictures later. She's heavy. Danny is honest to a fault. Her face is attractive, easy on the eyes. Her status is *in a relationship*. The *with* is not Danny Ray. I wonder if I would be bothered if it were. Her pictures are generic. Restaurants, baseball games, swimming pool shots, dogs, flowers, her and her boyfriend, Christmas, the usual. Danielle's life appears busy. No pictures of Danny. They are so white, like Christmas catalogue white. She seems classier than Danny.

I scan for clues. *Who is this person? Who are the people in his life? What are their social norms?* Danny describes his family's racist belief system as business as usual. I'm afraid to go to the hospital. I'm terrified of possible rejection and I'm terrified that no one he knows, knows exactly who I am. *What is the worst-case scenario?* His family may say, "don't come back, we hate niggers!" I don't like discomfort and this scenario would definitely make me uncomfortable.

I click back through Danny's friends. Out of the 900 plus, four are black, all four went to Crandall High. I sigh, closing my laptop. *These people aren't ready for my presence.* I wonder if this blind hatred they possess will show. I don't mind them rejecting my blackness. I just don't care to contend with it, especially if I don't have to.

A week has passed since Lonny called. He hasn't sent the text he promised, nor have I heard from Danny's mom through Lonny.

Why did Lonny have to tell me this? The heaviness of Danny's condition weighs on me. I want to walk away, cut my loses, avoid this truth. *Is Lonny telling the truth?* Danny did say Lonny was a liar. *If Danny wants to be done with me, why go through such major theatrics?* I know how to take a hint. I have been ghosted and have grossed, more than I care to remember.

Exactly seven days have passed. It's Monday morning. I ring Lonny with no answer. I leave a gentle message. My anxiety doesn't allow me to move on without some resolution or closure. Before the day is over I call the hospital. My desire to walk away is not stronger than some progressive desire within me to see it through. *Who am I and why does this matter to me?*

"Baylor Medical..." The operator answers.

"Hi...I'm calling to find out if you have a patient by the name of Danny Austin?"

"Let me see..." She draws out each word. I hear tapping on the keyboard in the background. This moment feels slow. I experience every ounce of the wait. Thirty seconds. I sit at my kitchen table unwrapping Starbursts. One red, one pink, one orange and one yellow. I place one on top of the other, smash them together and take a bite. I salivate deeply.

"Okay, here we are."

I swallow my tangy and sweet saliva.

"He's in ICU. His room number is 3602a. If you want to speak with someone there you'll have to call the ICU front desk. Do you need that number ma'am?" The cheerful operator asks.

I scribbled the info on an old utility bill. "No thank you. I have that number." We disconnect.

I make a plan to visit him in the morning. Lonny finally returns my call only to tell me that Danny is still in a coma. This isn't good.

Calling myself an introvert is possibly an understatement. I stand in front of my vanity, styling my hair. The clock on my smart phone reads eight am. I'm leaving in an hour. I figure visiting after ten am would ensure Danny's family and friends are at a minimum, and hopefully at work. I pop two Xanax before I leave. I have a third in the small pink pill case I keep inside my purse. I don't puff today.

I search my psyche for reasons why I'm not able to turn my back to this situation. *Why am I drawn to this?* I don't know much about Danny, but I do know that his favorite color is blue, as is mine. I stop at the Tom Thumb to grab some sort of gift. Flowers, a plant? I stand in the middle of the floral arrangements and it hits me. It hits me that I'm about to go to the hospital to visit someone I've only dated for two weeks and that I couldn't back out. I don't have a choice. Something more powerful than my rationale is taking the wheel. I'm frozen, staring at the most beautiful blue orchids I've ever laid eyes on. *You can't handle this. You're just a shy little girl. A late bloomer. You don't have the balls to go through with this. You don't care about people like this.* I exhale my negative self-talk away.

I phone my sister. She decided that morning to leave work early. I beg her to stand with me for moral support. She doesn't hesitate. I pick her up from her house about an hour later with a carefully selected card and the beautiful blue orchids I couldn't take my eyes off.

Danny often refers to his son as his little Superman. And when he wants to massage his own ego he calls himself Superman. I sign his card *To Superman.* I guess I know this about him too.

On the drive over to Baylor, my sister and I discuss the four dates. Up until now, these dates have been my precious little secrets. Sometimes food tastes better when you don't have to share. This is how I feel about my time spent with Danny. It's been about him and me discovering each other through our own eyes and not through the judgement of others. It's a quiet freedom.

We complain about how hard the building is to find, then we gripe about the cost of parking and finally bad mouth the choice of elevator placement throughout the building. These gripes are distractions. Underneath our querulous attitudes were puddles of fear, some deep some shallow. We try not to step in any. We avoid the puddles.

Once the elevator pauses on the third floor my stomach burns. I pop another Xanax. We're both silent. The bell dings and the doors open. The Xanax is barely keeping me together. My body likes panic attacks. It's begging for one.

The ICU is enamored with needs. Nurses run from one end of the three-way hallway to the next. There is a circular desk right in the middle where all three hallways meet. We stand there momentarily before someone notices us. One of the many nurses in matching scrubs and a ponytail stops abruptly.

"Has anyone helped ya'll yet?"

We stand stoically, side by side. I answer with a stutter. I swallow. "We're trying to find room 3602a." I forget about the way I feel for a moment. "Danny Austin?" I swallow again. Time moves fast, but my brain has slowed to a crawl, maybe the excitement, possibly the Xanax. She points at two large wooden, glass and metal doors.

"Ma'am, you can't bring that plant in there." She adds. I turn and place it on the circular desk. "You can leave it there and we'll give it to his family." The nurse pushes the orchid towards the middle of the desk. The orchids were also a distraction, I'm forced to let go.

We enter the double doors and then another door to the right that reads 3602a-h. The letters are for each individual bed, this room has eight. I've almost forgotten what Danny looks like in person. It's hard for me to picture someone's exact physical structure, with detail when I haven't been in their company. But I do know that I will know him when I see him.

The room is lit but shadowy. Two large windows to the back of the room, only one of the windows' blinds are cracked. Sheet-like curtains separate one patient from the other. Millennial aged nurses move about briskly from bed to bed, checking vitals and doing other medical maintenance. It feels crowded.

Within seconds I look to the right. I see Danny. For a split second I'm not sure if it is him. His head is heavily wrapped with gauze like coma victims on daytime soap operas.

Danny has a contraption around his skull. A metal halo. This is serious. The gauze is full of blood and topped off with a plastic helmet. His eyelids are blood shot and sealed shut. Two shiners. His nose is swollen around the bridge with breathing tubes inserted pass the swelling like trains barging through a slim tunnel. His mouth is free. He has bruises and stiches all over his body. One leg is in a brace and cast. This has happened, is happening. He is in the thick of it, and I am present.

Danny is in a coma. My sister is directly beside me. I look back at her and away from Danny. Like the way I was taught in film classes in college to cut away from intense action or extremely graphic scenes to give the viewer the mental space to process what they have just seen. I process. The look on my sister's face makes it real once again. What I witness hits me in waves. I check that this is no dream. I have vivid dreams, in color even. So deep, so often that I am regularly not sure if they are happening in real life or not.

Standing next to Danny's bed is his friend Davis from the construction site. He's short. Rugged face, Tom Selleck moustache. Blue collar. Danny is flailing about. His legs jolt around every few seconds. Davis wipes his mouth and holds down his legs.

"Hi...I'm Yasminah." I wait for his face to show a sign of remote familiarity, the black girl. It does. Danny has mentioned me. Davis grumbles a hello.

I walk closer to his bed. I reject a quick thought that he will not recover. This damage is grave. Davis explains his condition from head to toe. I'm in a haze. I only hear phrases. Medically induced coma, fractured skull, broken nose, crushed pelvis, metal rods, too early to tell, several more surgeries...his voice trails off. He and my sister share a cordial exchange. All I see is Danny. Poor tattered Danny.

I reach out to touch his hand. It flinches sporadically. He is responsive but not fully conscious.

"Has he spoke yet?" I ask Davis, not taking my eyes off Danny.

"Nothing yet. He's just been mumbling and moving non-stop. It's like he wants to get up but doesn't know what's going on." Davis sounds like King of the Hill too.

He leans down towards Danny's ear. He wipes Danny's mouth once more.

"It's Yasminah...Yasminah's here to see you...do you understand me?" Davis waits. Danny begins to flail his arms around. Davis holds him down with one hand.

"Yas....mi....nah!" Danny forced out each syllable of my name.

"He said my name..." I whisper loudly and smile big. I'm touched. Danny's hard drive has a hairline fracture, the data has been compromised but it's still there.

His eyes are still shut. His legs flailing about. He wants out of this nightmare but can't come to.

"Well look at that..." Davis adds, his Tom Selleck stache barely shifting. "That's the first time he's been that clear."

My sister smiles through the tears she's collected, seemingly suddenly. This is real.

The rest of Danny's family is in the waiting room. His mom, aunt, uncle, Tim's mom, nieces, nephews and cousins. We slip by all of them without effort, our meeting is not meant for this day or any future day, for that matter. I ditch my recurring fantasy of the worst-case scenario and focus on Danny. This is bigger than his family's racist beliefs. I feel I'm needed here. *But in what way?*

I wonder for a moment if Davis will tell the rest of them I stopped by. I wonder why I care. I run my finger across the backside of Danny's scaly hand. Fresh construction calluses. I feel it is just about time to leave. To leave unseen, unjudged and unoffended. I know this is not the end of this. Danny is a cowboy, a renegade, scrappy, a do whatever it takes to win, kind of guy. Invincible. How can this be?

We wrap it up when the nurse returns to check his vitals and administer more medication. It's apparent we are not family and it isn't visiting hour time. I'm so happy we didn't know, and I got this over with. I force all of the breath out of me, from the pit of my stomach. I clear the few remaining butterflies that flutter down below. I recall a first-grade field day with my oldest where she began to cry on the playground and one of her male classmates says, "breathe...take deep belly breaths and you'll be okay!" He took a deep breath himself to support, placing his hand on her shoulder. They were six. One more deep breath and we're on the elevators heading back to the car. *I did it.*

Danny lay in his medically induced coma for another week, then another, and another. After three weeks, I text Lonny. I search my brain for a way out of caring, but none seem plausible. For days Lonny doesn't respond. *Am I no longer welcomed at the hospital since I didn't go through the proper channels? What are proper channels for relationships that aren't properly defined?*

My daughters are on vacation with family, so I plan a retreat of my own to Port Aransas. I search the web for the best beaches in Texas, a state not exactly known for its surfeit of sandy, blue beaches. I eventually find what the locals refer to as, Port A. A smidge under 200 miles away from the Mexican border. South Texas. The Gulf of Mexico.

I invite along a friend. Three days, in the heat, sand and salty water. I plan to visit Danny before my trip. I call the hospital to see if he is still in the coma, and in the ICU. The ICU receptionist gives me a new room number and new visiting hours.

I want to visit, but every fiber of my being radiates with teeny tiny balls of fire. They bounce aggressively from one end of my body to the other. The subtle yet chaotic storm rolls through me like a wave of sporadic water bubbles in a pot of boiling water, fighting with fervor to reach the surface. To be free. It begins in the pit of my gut, pushing down first through my intestine and then directly to my chest. My heart sprints, pumping blood through my extremities, my under arms feel hot. Every pit on my body tingles and itches. Arm pits, hip pits, knee pits. I breathe deep, attempting to flush this away. My fingertips tremble, they feel electric. I swallow deep. The heat moves to my anus. It itches first. And then it sweats.

Fucking anxiety. This volcano is frequently on the verge of eruption. So I puff.

My plan is to visit the hospital the morning of my road trip to Port A. The night before I leave, I stop at the local Family Dollar store to pick up a few last-minute travel items. Toothbrush, deodorant and a gift for Danny. I don't feel sad or bad, but I feel vested.

I come alive perched on warm sand, absorbing the sun and listening with perfect attention to the ocean's song. Not a note out of key.

Leslie is ready. I tell her they'll be one last stop before I pick her up.

"Stopping by to see Danny?" Leslie asks over the phone.

"Yes...I just don't want to leave without dropping off my gift." I reply, with little enthusiasm.

"Let's hope he gets this one. The blue orchid just disappeared." I add, rolling my eyes. Leslie giggles at the mystery of it all.

I want to giggle too but I watch my body instead. Two-thirds attention to my body and one-third attention to Leslie. I'm waiting for the signs of the anxiety to subside. The itching stops first, then the sweat beads evaporate, then the over-whelming desire to shit dwindles and last; the stomach ache retreats. I'm still racked with paranoia, but my body doesn't react. This is good. *Fucking anxiety.* Leslie and I are quiet for too many consecutive moments. So, I let her go.

My gift, the superman blanket is electric blue, fiery red and golden yellow. The Superman logo is repeated for as long and wide as the blanket. Its soft and snuggly. I fold it neatly and place it into a deep gift bag. I pull out of my driveway and with each passing moment the gift begins to feel like overkill. "Do I seem like a stalker?" "What will his family think of me?" "Why am I so compelled to stick around?" "I don't even want to stick around." I whisper these phrases.

I get on the interstate, moving in the direction of the hospital. I'm in a daze mostly. No anxiety that I can feel, the pill is working. I'm just numb but below my surface the there is still turmoil; like a hidden current beneath the surface of a calm lake. I see the exit and I pass it. I don't hesitate or vacillate; my day has a different path in mind. I'm carried away by a strong energetic force. Brining Danny this blanket is not on my list, so I don't force it, I just wait.

I have no desire to pull a *While You Were Sleeping*. I think, *I should ignore this. Ignore him. He's not my man. He's not even my type.*

Before these thoughts fully process, I'm already on my way to Leslie.

Sweet, bubbly Leslie. Wouldn't hurt a fly. I then wonder if she could be a sociopath. That thought flashes quickly. People would dislike most people if they only knew the quick thoughts others had about them for no good reason. I picture my gay professor having sex sometimes, and him being a bottom. When I'm people watching, I picture couples having nasty fights with each other behind closed doors. I picture the men on their knees begging for a woman's forgiveness.

In my head, I call everyone a bitch, even men, when I'm in that mood. I smile, but I think *"bitch!"*. Leslie is not a bitch. Not openly anyway. She often makes me wonder who she really is. Leslie is a devout Christian. I don't share my pot habit with her or my sex talk.

JAMEELAH RAOOF

CHAPTER NINE

Port A

Leslie and I arrive in Port A. We take in the quaint beach houses, the Confederate flags on display and the golf carts sharing the road with real cars. Quietly, we scan for black people. Just because. This routine to find likeness is unspoken. We inherited the routine of seeking out blacks everywhere we go.

After winning at a game of wits against the office manager, we retreat to our room. The office manager tries to charge us more, makes me prove we don't owe the money and all the while I make sure I never lose my cool. I don't feel like being their *black girl* stereotype. I don't flinch because I'm right. Rightness doesn't need theatrics. Leslie... Leslie is class personified. In this moment I am happy this is the friend I chose.

This office manager is obnoxious. The level of her outrageous treatment shocks both Leslie and me. We glance at each other with our eyes stretched. We can't afford to be human. We know we'll be black first, and with no other blacks in sight, we can't afford to be the universal representation by telling this manager how despicable her behavior is. This is understood between Leslie and I, but unspoken. I hate feeling I need to be something else in white spaces. This fact sucks. Fucking Racism. To be honest, I'm not sure if the office manager is bat shit crazy, racist or both. I choose not to decide. I exhale, feel arrogant in my rightness, watch her retreat into her wrongness and say, "thank you, have a beautiful day." She puts the keys on the counter and walks away.

Leslie and I discuss this incident, share how floored we are by such a bad attitude, then of course skedaddle off to the beach. We don't acknowledge the possibility of racism out loud. Something about that hurts.

The beach. Oh...it is beautiful. So much depth. The sand is hot. We happily drudge towards the waves. The waves. They are constant. They have character. They do what they are designed to do, each crest original. Never repeating, but always the same.

"This is beautiful...I've never been to the ocean..." Leslie whispers. The waves are loud. The wind bangs against our afro puffs.

"It's actually the gulf..." I wonder why I had to say this as it falls off my tongue.

I correct everybody, aloud and in my head. *Is the gulf the same as the ocean?* This thought distorts my view. I go from majestic feelings to resembling an encyclopedia.

Three days of yoga on the beach, only limited talk about men and limitless talk about hopes, dreams, and yoga technique.

On the last day, while we gather our belongings off the sand, a huge pick-up truck barrels down the beachfront road. It displays two large confederate flags on flag poles, on both sides of the vehicle. The driver is wearing no shirt, is drinking beer, is playing loud country music, is white and is unbothered. The driver shouts something inaudible topped off with a "whooohoooo!" I don't like to acknowledge racism, but my connection with Danny Ray has put these thoughts at the forefront of my mind.

The thought of the road trip back home wears on my mental a bit. It's the driving, its leaving the beach, its missing my daughters; all in one emergent package.

One hour into our trip I am a million miles deep in my galaxy. I don't listen to music when I drive, I let my imagination make movies, speeches, edit my personal historical events and rehearse my future encounters. I often have sex in these movies. Sex is perfect in my movies. Real life sex is never as good as the sex in my mental movies. My sub-conscious and conscious mind do the tango as I drive, they romance each other. I'm there but I'm not. Leslie is here too.

My phone rings. The screen says Danny. I watch it. My mind is trying to catch up with the why and the how. I finally answer.

"Hello..."

"Yasminah... It's Danny!" He shouts in his high-pitched, squirrely voice.

It's him.

"Hey... how are you...I mean when did you..." I lose my words, but not my thoughts. This encounter was not rehearsed in my movies. I'm fixed on my lack of preparation. I realize in this moment, I thought he would not out live his coma. It's been six weeks. It's like a movie. Leslie's eyes light up. This is impactful. I'm adrift in the middle of the ocean with my only option being to let go and see what happens. This moment is not in my control. This feels rare and I occupy a starring role in it.

"It's me Danny Ray..." He is clear, lucid.

"Well...how are you? When did you wake up?" I mock a concerned tone. I'm concerned but I don't have a predetermined tone for it, so I make one.

"This morning...I can't talk long. My mom told me you came by. She said Davis met you and your sister." Danny squawks. His words freely pouring out.

"I have a gift for you I want to drop off." I slide in, in between Danny's excitement.

"You can bring it today, visiting hours are still going on." Danny is eager. His life was on hold, and he doesn't like that he missed any of it.

"Actually, I'm in Port A." I feel uncategorizable when I say this because only white people talk about going to Port A. I'm not basic, and now he knows there is more to me than my blackness. I like to make sure of it. I'm probably stacking.

"I love Port A. It's a great beach!" Danny adds, authentic and enthusiastic.

I realize the mental picture of him I hold is Danny without bandages, without bruises, without casts on both arms. He is physically whole in my imagination.

"I can bring it when I get back, me and my friend Leslie are on the road back to Dallas right now." I feel a little excited. I'm still floating in the middle of that ocean, still letting go.

"Okay...well the doctor just came in to take me to run more tests, just call me when you get back." Danny closes out the phone call.

We disconnect.

"Wow!" I glance over at Leslie. "Six weeks and he just wakes up talking like that?!"

"It's happened before." She adds.

"To who? This is rare." I interject.

"Rare but not impossible..." Leslie has a calm that welcomes miracles. She doesn't require an explanation.

My shock occupies more than a few moments. I prolong this. This happening is a high-note in my life. In between these high-notes are calm, boredom, waiting, anticipating, longing. This is a main event. I choose to engulf myself in its mystique.

JAMEELAH RAOOF

CHAPTER TEN

Gail and Deborah

Danny has two moms, he once confessed on one of our dates. Actually, it was the date where we sat at the bar all night and chatted at Top Golf. He talked about his mom and his aunt and how they do everything for him. Cook for him, clean for him, run errands for him, etc. He divulges this with a sly grin. I'm not surprised. He has definiteness of purpose. When a will is strong and sure, it mostly takes and others mostly allow. Danny is good at taking and letting women allow.

I have three college degrees. I'm a college professor. I own my own home. It is better and bigger than Danny's. I own my car. I was raised responsibly. *How can I not be good enough for a railroad worker? Even a white railroad worker.*

These women will be at the hospital when I visit. They will try their best to get over my brown skin. They will be embarrassed of my presence. They do not think a black girl is good enough for Danny. I think.

After returning from Port A, I feel refreshed. I have control issues and Danny Ray's presence is forcing me to address them. Anger issues too. Anxiety issues and now racial issues. A topic I avoid often. Not because it hurts. I don't like being typical. Now the topic of race is suddenly something I must face down.

Same hospital, different room, no ICU, now recovery. He's in another wing of the hospital. A wing dedicated to those who have suffered traumatic brain injury. I pop two Xanax on the drive over. I puffed before I left. I want my head to be gone. I need to be lifted above any criticism.

I feel floaty, more high than usual like I'm actually floating. I drive perfectly whether I'm high or not. I pull into the parking lot, squirt eye drops in both eyes, pop in a stick of gum and proceed to conquer the upcoming moments.

I float through the entrance, huge, glass double doors. They fly open at the slightest provocation. A bird flies low and they shoot open before I get there. The café filled with restless family members is directly off the entrance. Danny texted me the address and location. I check my messages to find my destination again. I am unbothered. Either the Xanax or the pot is working better than expected. I don't even question why I'm going through with seeing him again. I think...*why not?* I'm on an adventure. I get to see how this plays out. I get to watch the reactions of these women from the outside in. I'm no longer bogged down by what role I play. I am watching Yasminah from a far, up close. She will be fine.

The elevator door opens to Danny's floor. I have not rehearsed what his room looks like, or how it smells, or how it feels. This story is building with each step I take. This story reveals a new world inside of me. It has always existed, lying dormant. New land yet to be cultivated. I am curious. I open myself in a way I had never achieved or attempted in the past. This march through the hospital corridor is orgasmic and I explode with anticipation.

I reach what could be best described as a cul-de-sac consisting of three separate rooms in a half-circle, adjacent to the circular reception area. I look over into one of the three the rooms. I see a family, an overweight man with tubes connected to his nose and an IV stand beside his bed. He struggles to sit up. Something about seeing people near death or in a near death scare is intriguing. Death is the grand finale. Seeing sick people lets me get close to it, fondle it a bit, dip the tip of my big toe into the puddle of death without having to get wet. With Danny, I will get wet.

The door is cracked, I knock. Aunt Deborah is bright, healthy and light. Gail is dark, older, unhappy. They are sisters, and these are their roles. Gail's troubles weigh her down externally but, Deborah's do not. I step forward and release my snap judgement.

Danny shuffles to attention when I step in. I have my phone in one hand and the little gift bag with his superman blanket in the other. His blood shot eyes, lit up, happy to see me. He no longer has the head bandage or the metal halo. Both arms are in a cast and also one leg. He looks agile and healthy.

Gail is chatting with the nurse and Deborah is changing the TV stations. They don't look surprised that I'm here. Deborah smiles, rises and introduces herself. Danny is distracted by his mom and the nurse. I am enjoying everyone's focus being divided. *Do I look high?* I ask myself. I'm feeling great.

The nurse smiles at me as she exits the room. It's just us. Gail turns to me, masks her bleakness with charm. It's mostly convincing.

"Momma that's Yasminah, Yasminah that's my momma...oh and Aunt Deborah..." Danny's eyes float away from his mom and towards his aunt. He grins big in my direction.

I'm wearing a simple, soft pink summer dress, lace, eyelets, and cotton... Danny's eyes survey my body. He looks pleased.

The hospital is busy. There is action, buzzing, a flow of energy. Danny's bed is on the diagonal, the shower is a walk-in attached to the toilet. His room feels warm and like a home.

"Sit...Momma move, make some space for..." Danny is excited like a kid. He's antsy like a kid and coddled like a kid.

He stutters, "...make some space for Yasminah..."

Danny is experiencing memory loss and had been since he awoke from his coma. He doesn't remember his fall, but he remembers me. *I wonder if he remembers not calling me before he fell?* I think right now this isn't important.

I sit beside his bed. I've met his mother and aunt. White hair, sixty plus average Texan, white women, fitted in Chico's, Steinmart, and Ann Taylor.

I try to look beyond his double casted arms, propped up by a pole, a pole attached to an apparatus wrapped around his waist. He's bounded.

I hand over the superman blanket. His mother and aunt dote over it. They recall his constant referral to himself as the super hero.

Gail holds the blanket in the air. This is all surreal. I fight the desire to question why I'm even here. These are not my people of comfort. I am on foreign turf, in unexplored lands. I think what my family members might say, then I put those thoughts down in order to engage.

I smile, I appear humble and sweet to them. Sweeter than I actually am. Truth is, Danny is a bit of an asshole and so am I. He is attracted to my sweetness because he is seen as so abrasive. But he is not all that abrasive and I am not all that sweet. These are our outer shells. We both wear them well. I like my role here. In none of my other worlds am I seen this way.

"So, what do you do Yasminah?" Deborah asks as she tucks the superman blanket around the edges of Danny's bed. She moves slowly around his casted leg.

"I'm a computer science professor..." I reply. I wait for the shock and praise. I get it each time I say what I do. I am often in uncommon places for black women, so I get this often. I get this at work, I get this at yoga, I get this at my daughters' school, I get this at my daughters' ballet class. I get this a lot.

She stops in her tracks. "Well, you're just a whiz, aren't you?" Her eyes light up. This particular phrase is a first. *I'm a whiz.*

I nod with a soft grin, at least I think it's a soft grin, I'm still high. Its fading but I check my mental faculties and the high is still there. I shock and intimidate as usual. I don't need to stack high with Danny's people. Education is a foreign notion to them. They are relics from the blue-collar, undereducated, but still well-paid era; especially as it pertained to white men and their families.

Danny's mom is making little eye contact with me. She doesn't like my presence, but in this moment she is more afraid of her son not making a full recovery. For now, his condition one-ups my blackness.

"Well, we'll let ya'll have some privacy." Gail decides, Deborah scrambles and follows. They leave a slight crack in the door. The television is low. It buffers our awkwardness, the soft mumble of the TV is like a homegirl you drag with you on a blind date, our welcomed third wheel.

It also buffers the silent spaces our lack of friendship does not allow us to fill. I look at Danny with both arms in casts, hoisted up high. He cannot do for himself. I don't want to date him in this instance, I want to friend him. I feel I am needed. My friendship feels like a necessary aspect of his healing. He needs to know that someone is there for him who is not obligated to be.

"I didn't think you were coming." He chuckles. I feel his shame of remembering that he didn't call. He searches my face to see if I remember, to see if I'm holding this against him. But I am not. It is easy for me to be here. It seems the only place I should be, in this moment, at this time. This is a part of my story. I don't see the next step but today, this is the space I should be filling. Right here, at a hospital, in the long-term facility ward, next to Danny's bed.

I move past his ghosting. I have been the giver and the receiver of ghosting on more than one occasion, this does not ruin me.

"Of course, I'd come..." I reply glancing toward the television. Lingering eye contact could mean I'm there for romantic reasons, so I purposely don't linger. "I tend to do what I say I'm going to do." I add.

"A lot of people say they're going to do things and don't do them. I'm waiting for Lonny's worthless ass to pay me back my money right now. He's lucky I'm in the hospital. But I will be home soon." He gripes, then flashes his go-to toothy grin.

I just listen.

"I should be back at work soon. I already called my boss. I should be back in a few weeks." Danny spouts. He flagrantly ignores the depth of his condition. His ocean blue eyes glance up at the television.

I decide to be with him in that belief, no matter how misguided. "That will be good." I reply.

He smiles and stares at me.

"What?" I giggle, thinking how fun it is to be watched.

"Damn you're beautiful." He adds.

I giggle again, because this I already know.

We chat about his fall. He claims to not remember any of the events of that day. I can only relate this to restoring the system to an earlier date on a computer. After working in IT and teaching computer science, I relate everything to computers without even thinking. The computer doesn't forget everything, just the events of the days you choose. I sometimes wonder if we choose to forget trauma or is this the only way our mental computer can be salvaged. The only way we can make sense of life and move forward. Some events are so traumatic that they defy reason. Since we can't comprehend that reason, we archive it and retrieve it only when life requires us to. Right now, Danny does not need it, he needs to know that he will be okay. My presence whispers to him that despite his physical condition, he is still okay.

Shortly after, his mother and aunt return to the room with one large McDonald's bag for Danny. I boycotted that particular fast-food establishment years ago and have never looked back. The smell of the infamous french-fries fills the room. Aunt Deborah is happy to bring Danny something he loves. She sits next to him and begins to peel the waxy yellow wrapper back from around the burger. Danny has tunnel vison. Nothing exists in this moment but his double cheeseburger. His eyes salivate. Aunt Deborah reaches over to feed Danny the burger and he nearly bites her hand off. I think, *he is wild, and they are used to it.* The burger never had a chance.

After watching with curiosity as Danny inhales his lunch in only a few bites, I feel the inkling to leave. I don't leave immediately. In yoga, it is said that the moment you are ready to leave the pose is when the practice actually begins. As an introvert, I leave everything when that inkling hits. My high is wearing off.

My children are with their extended family and I have the rest of this day to myself, to be with myself. But I stay. I stay pass the discomfort and I breathe. They make small talk about the hospital and the staff. They do their best to stay on task. The task being, don't make a big deal out of her presence. My presence. Danny's request for my company smooths over the rough spots. They are nice to me. Danny's mom and aunt were bred to be nice. They're good at it. They don't reject me, instead it seems they're trying to understand how they should feel about me. *Does she want something?* I think, while mentally acknowledging that I could be wrong. What will people say if they see her when they visit?

The nurse enters, and she is like a cold glass of water complete with beads of dripping condensation after a mid-summer hike in Texas. It is not unbearable, but the water is a relief. Sweet appreciated relief.

"We need to get some x-rays of Danny's hand." She states while checking off some items on her clipboard. It's apparent that we're on *her* time now; the urgency has shifted. This is my chance to retreat.

I feel Danny's mom and aunt want to put me in that cube, but everything about me screams I don't belong there. They don't know where to put me. This makes me feel like I'm better. Danny's mom and aunt can't conceive my vastness, my depth. This is pleasing. I leave, Danny's attention has shifted too. He is stuck in a physical shape that does not provide freedom, but he is moving. His demand to live a free life pushes the nurses around, and his mom and aunt. Like a speedboat racing across a lake, just like the way the water parts, they move for him.

I slip out of their way as the nurse and his mom help load Danny into his wheelchair. He follows my face once he is in the chair to see if I see him as less, but I don't. I give a half hug to Danny and say good bye. He hollers, "I'll text you!"

I step onto to the elevator and a feeling comes over me that I have never truly felt. It feels like bravery. I think, *I feel brave.* While there are many events and undertakings in my life I have been called brave for, like moving to other states with no money, going to Puerto Rico with Rogelio or going through with my divorce, they did not take bravery. Not for me. Those things felt like the only choice. Necessity is not bravery, it is necessity. Visiting Danny and visualizing his mother having a panic attack pointing while shouting, *"Oh my lord...as I stand here in my living flesh...she is a black woman, call the governor, my lord she is a black woman!"* With a Texas twang of course. In my forethought, Gail is shouting this in the lobby, while fainting with the back of one hand over her forehead and the other hand clinching her heart, falling backwards into the arms of his aunt. This did not happen. The sky did not fall, hell did not freeze over and pigs did not fly. I was brave. And it seems, regardless of their feelings, they were too.

I make it to my car, I don't even contemplate returning. My artificial high has been replaced with an unwavering natural one. I bask in this feeling for the remainder of my day.

CHAPTER ELEVEN

No Good Racist Bastards

Danny sends me a text, thanking me for showing up. I think, *I can show up, I'm good at showing up.* I know he can't text himself, so someone else is showing up for him too, even if they are reluctant to do so.

I speak with my brother later that night over the phone. Before I could say a word, he says, "Tell me all about it, tell me what those no good racist bastards did to you." I shout in laughter. If you know my brother, you would know that he possesses excellent comedic timing and a profound ability to never seem as though he takes anything too seriously. Throughout my tumultuous relationship that ultimately led up to my divorce, he kept me laughing at my ex, our mothers and myself each step of the way. This adventure is no different.

"Hush!" I shout as I calm my laughter. He laughs too. We enjoy the type of dark comedy you can only share with a true friend or a soul-mate. My laughter sums up my experience, the details can be fetched at a later date. The summation is all he is asking for. He makes sure his sister is okay, and I am.

I return to Danny's bedside by request two days later. Gail and Deborah are there being moved energetically by Danny, who is like a force of nature. I don't go through the mental phases of uncovering comfort, layer by layer. I grab my comfort and sit. Danny lays a path for me. A path that curves right around his mother and aunt. This is all I need to feel free.

Danny is very talkative today. He demands to go outside since the weather is permitting. He makes consistent effort to move past his condition. He asks me to take him outside, but Deborah sets aside her niceties and demands to take him herself. She offers nicely, but she is not requesting. For reasons unclear, she doesn't seem to trust me alone with him.

Danny has undergone two surgeries on his right hand and is planned for another the following day. Our visit today is to be short in order for him to prepare for this procedure.

We make it outside and Danny squirms around, giving orders to his aunt about which way to turn him, how fast he should go and the direction he wants to face. I sit on a bench and Deborah sits beside me.

"So, you said you teach computer science?" Deborah asks. I almost forget I mentioned this. My first visit is already a blur.

"Yes..." I add.

"For how long?" Deborah asks, almost automatically. The empty pleasantries continue.

"About seven years?" I nod.

Deborah reminds me of the women I've worked with, the clerical women at the colleges, or like the women at the electrical company manning the phones, or like my neighbors. She is familiar. Her way of being is familiar.

"She has two daughters... they go to private school, I can't even afford that." He adds. Danny responds to all of my luxuries in life with an air of shock that I can do what he can't. He doesn't hear this, but I do. My daughters do not go to private school. I don't correct him because I am too busy enjoying looking better. Danny stacks for me. I'm not sure if he is proud or issuing a disclaimer. *She's not like the black women we see on tv, she's better than that, see!* Aunt Deborah is impressed. It works.

Listening to them converse about no good Lonny and how he hasn't come to visit or pay Danny back money he owes him, feels like King of the Hill again. If they were real people and not animated. Their twang is so strong. It is not always present. I think, *this must be the country white version of code switching. Fixin' to... ain't gonna...* or *fot* instead of fight. I am unapologetically amused.

On my forth visit to see Danny this white space has transformed into Danny and I's space. He puts everything secondary to seeing me. His mother and aunt scoots quickly out of the way when I arrive. They stop guarding him. I began to take Danny for his outside strolls, he only wants me to take him.

Our conversations gain no more depth and are not particularly suspenseful. It feels we are enamored by our unlikely presence in each other's journey. Him, a wild mustang who used the N word as a common name for blacks in his youth and me a tamed professor who had been raised on the premise of being better than and staying clear of the *white devil.* The devil is supposed to be scary. Danny does not scare me. I feel I should be outraged. I should run for the hills. Danny does not deserve my presence but instead I am drawn in. He seems less white and more Danny, with every encounter.

I hover above this woman, Yasminah, who helps this man put his life back together and she does not plan on moving on until her work is done. She is not capable of feeling the pain of her ancestors or his. She is writing a new story moved by something much larger than herself. Our connection is pure, clean, without hesitance or distraction. It's not tainted by expectations. Each day is a new day, and we choose to be friends each day. It is easy. Easy feels too sweet to release. I have never felt this ease in any relationship, no demands to change or pressure to be something I am not. Both of us know deep inside this may not have any future. With no future, the present is new, enough, and real.

Danny decides he wants his hair cut. He requests through text that I bring clippers if I have them. Of course, I don't, but I buy some. When I arrive this day, it is like a madhouse. Danny has his full upper body cast removed and only the arm and hand where his surgeries are taking place is in a cast. Danny fell on his right side, shattering everything on that side of his body. He is fighting the process, of going slow enough not to do any new damage to his body. With every swift movement he makes all the women in the room hover and brace for the worst.

Gail pulls me aside this day. "You know he's not all the way there. If he texts you and says something he shouldn't it's because his brain ain't quite functioning as it should. Tim hasn't come to see him again. I think it's hard for Tim to see his daddy like this. Danny is so strong and active that this is killing him more than he admits. And Danielle can't do anything with Tim, the teacher says he's being disrespectful. Danny won't be able to go back to work anytime soon and he just keeps bothering his boss." Gail hammers on with the same sadness she's held since I met her. It draws her face south, tugging downward both her skin and the corners of her eyes.

I listen. This day I am not high. I experience her sadness through her words and her face without my filter. For a quick second, I think, this is the same woman that playfully answered her phone with her kids saying, "you're a nigger and I'm not." Like a game of tag, who could be tagged as the worst type of person first. A nigger. In other words, *I may be a lot of things but thank God I'm not nigger.*

What could she possibly need from me? Acceptance, reassurance, forgiveness? I just listen. To her am I now the good kind of nigger I suppose? White spaces confuse me. They are formed around pretenses that no one seems enjoy, not even the ones who create and facilitate them. White spaces garner white fear, fear of the *others* and fear of themselves.

Lots of Danny's old self has returned. He makes crass jokes about sex in front of his mom and laughs at the way she squirms. He is completely uninhibited. He makes light of challenging the constrained social practices of others, especially those close to him. The madhouse is centered around Danny having to take a shower and trying to do it himself. Both Aunt Deborah and the nurse are standing by as he fights to get up from the chair, grabbing hold of the handicap shower bar. They brace themselves, anticipating his fall like new mothers do when babies are learning to walk. He is naked. I have ample opportunity to check out his package just for kicks, but I choose not to. I step outside and wait.

When Danny is ready, I return with my clippers. He says, "Okay...you can cut it now."

I laugh. "What makes you think I know how to use clippers?"

Danny looks confused. "A black guy I work with says he cuts his own hair."

I reply, "On average, it's quite the opposite. Black barbershops are huge." I can see from his expression the fact that the one black guy he knows from work doesn't represent all black men is mind boggling. When Danny says the word black, Gail and Deborah recoil, they hold their breath until they're sure he hasn't disrupted the ecosystem. It's like, we know she's black, but we don't have to acknowledge it when she's around. Or something like that.

He wants his hair shaved off to a buzz cut, military style. Since his accident, he has lost a considerable amount of weight. This look he wants gives off the skinhead vibe. Danny turns to the nurse and asks if she's cut hair before, she says no. He turns to his Aunt and asks if she's cut hair before, she says no. Everybody is chuckling but Danny. He turns back to me and says, "Well you do it." I draw back. He says, "We'll put a guard on it and you can't mess it up." I want to be as confident as I appear. I step between the women crowding the small space and say, "Okay!"

"Are you sure Danny?" Aunt Deborah says politely, looking pass me.

"I trust Yasminah." Danny adds.

The women step out of the small bathroom and for the next ten minutes there was only silence and the buzz of the clippers. Cutting his hair felt good. It felt powerful. Before long I was a pro. As I turn off the clippers, the vibration still lingering in my hands match the exhilaration on my insides. I feel first and trusted. Before I leave the restroom, I wipe the smirk off my face.

For the next couple of weeks, I visit Danny regularly. His recovery is a legend. The doctors have no idea how this man survived a thirty-foot fall to the concrete and has seemingly no brain damage. He is sharp. During our visits, we play dominoes often. I am the only one who beats Danny. He says he doesn't mind losing to me. Gail and Deborah began to look forward to my visits. When I arrive they say, "...there she is!" and smile.

Danny has managed to piss so many people off from his past with his crass comments, belligerent drunkenness, and tendency to streak at parties; that almost no one has visited. This reminds me of the funeral test. You know you're living a good life when people would care if you died. With

Danny, it seems, not so much. He is exhausting to those he takes for granted. Each time his jokes go too far or his tongue is too vulgar he glances at me to see if I approve. I'm not moved either way.

Danny's spirits are high, always high. The doctors tell him he has to go to a long-term facility for a month to learn to walk on his leg again and to use his right hand. This is the only time I ever see hopelessness in Danny's eyes. Seeing him this way was akin to the feeling I get when I hurt my daughters in that deep way, not when they're upset about a toy they can't have, but when I unintentionally say something that cuts through their armor and empties them out the way only a mother could. This feeling stinks.

Danny heads to Irving. I tell him to text me when he arrives. He does not.

JAMEELAH RAOOF

CHAPTER TWELVE

Computer Nerd

Since there is no word from Danny, I dive back into yoga and back into myself. I don't want him for my man, but I find it hard to believe that he would risk our friendship by not calling. I don't contact him either. I wonder if he is okay. If his brain condition grew worse. If he wants to contact me but can't. I wrestle with these possibilities, but I cannot afford to give him the benefit of the doubt. I don't want to. Past scars of putting the well-being of men first will not allow me to, like an invisible but very real resistance band. I pull my thoughts back each time they veer in that direction.

My sister asks about Danny and since I'd forgiven his disappearing act before I don't mention this, I just say, "he's fine...doing great..." She likes fairytales, so this explanation is barely enough for her, I get by and through this conversation unscathed outwardly, but inwardly I feel like a fool.

I'm in my 9:00 am yoga class. This class is full. I tip-toe around the already stretched out mats, yogis marking their territory like puppies in heat. These women are serious about yoga. I glance around the room and wonder how yoga became such an upper-class white woman sport. And when I say sport, I do mean sport. They're not in it for the relaxation, the deeper connection to their inner-being, they are in these classes to be worked to depletion, like hamsters on a wheel, they never tire. These bitches are angry. Working off all that stay-at-home mom, desperate housewife anger. This is really not yoga. They are thin framed, ponytail donning, Lululemon maniacs. Any instructor that does not offer a minimum of twenty chaturangas a class be damned, the class size will dwindle.

My yoga studio is a white space and I am invisible here. I feel invisible not inferior. While I know that inferiority is often taught at home first, through comments like, "no matter how much a black man has, he's still a nigger," or "they think all of us come from poverty," etc., this country does provide plenty of real-life evidence of the superior/inferior relationship Black Americans share with White America. So, I choose invisible over inferior any day. And that's how I see it, my choice.

My desire to wear bold and brightly colored tights may or may not have something to do with this. Whenever I am noticed before class it's, "I love your tights and I love your hair..." after class it's, "You have a beautiful practice." I smile graciously, thinking quietly, *I know.* I practice on the front row because most women are too shy to. It's easy to be better in this white space. To be better in any space, you analyze the social characteristics, the unspoken values that govern that space and then be the one who displays all the characteristics they have the least of. Insecurity governs this space. These women all want to be liked. I negate being liked for being the least insecure. For me, admiration is better than popularity, although both can be lonely. Besides, if someone does talk to me, I only see it as an opportunity to stack, to sucker punch their cube of stories.

After class is over, the older woman next to me compliments my head stands. The instructor walks by and says, "isn't she a work of art?" I smile. When I am noticed in this space, I am often not human, I am not like them, I am instead, art. This might explain why many black women complain of whites wanting to touch their hair, because they know they're being seen as an inanimate object, something to covet, something not exactly human. In this context, *art* feels like another word for *other*. *Otherness* is exhausting.

I am waist-deep in the field of Information Technology. I have been working in this field since college. An amazing black professor by the name of Dr. Lainey Suleman, who has since passed away, saw a level of potential in me, that up until then, no one in my life had managed to tap into. She offered me a tech support position in her computer lab. Dr. Suleman taught me how to build computers and websites, edit video, network systems and many other tasks I could bore someone with at any given moment. She built websites for the government in the 1960s and worked as a head technology consultant for Microsoft. She was a badass. If anyone knew what white spaces were like, it was her. She convinced me that being in information technology as a black woman would make people's heads spin. She was a pro at stacking, her favorite phrase she would add to any conversation about me becoming a certified computer nerd was, "turning heads and changing perceptions." Dr. Suleman was all about the shock and awe. She loved technology as if it were her baby and you were special if she let you get close to her baby. I was special.

Ultimately, Dr. Suleman was right. After leaving college and attaining my first IT job, for the next decade, I never have the pleasure of working with another black woman again.

Information Technology, in this country, is a white space and even deeper, a white male space. Blind confidence, earth-shattering arrogance, and privilege. These men have the privilege of appearing to be smart just because they are white and male and mostly, wear glasses. They are exclusive, just like the stay-at-home, Lululemon mommies of yoga, either you fit, or you don't.

In any space I step into, I feel an overwhelming energy that drives the environment. At work, It's not always the work. Often, it's formal education, prestige, happiness, anger, race, beauty or money. Beneath all of these social displays commonly lies fear. With these white men, the overwhelming energy is rejection, a sort of underdog mindset. All of these men had been rejected for being computer nerds and going to technical school instead of university, but now, they have power. Revenge of the Nerds. The more educated, the more prestigious, the more beautiful, the smarter; all have to wait on them. Nothing moves until IT moves. They are the poster boys for computer knowledge. They have the Bill Gates look, which in this white space is akin to being a supermodel on the high-fashion runways of Milan.

Early on, I had been promoted to a higher-level support position at the main office of our employer. This promotion was strictly on merit. I couldn't miss any questions on the technology assessment portion of the interview. I couldn't afford not to know *all* the answers. Dr. Suleman did prepare me mentally for this. She told me that the bar for me in this industry would be set extra high, because they all want to know how you manage to infiltrate their exclusive, all white, all male, IT club. On several occasions, I'd stand next to a new IT guy, training him or showing him the ropes, and if an employee walked by asking a complex question related to their computer, they would turn their back to me assuming I couldn't help, as the new guy's glasses fog and cheeks fill with strawberry hued blotches, looking baffled before eventually pointing in my direction. It takes a while for me to understand this phenomenon. At that time in my life, I mostly dismiss race on a daily basis but that didn't mean the world did. Race is like a shackle around my neck, always pulling me back into its sorted web, no matter how much I choose to live beyond it. It yanks at my shirttail like a whiny kid begging for attention, oblivious to the disruption it beckons. It is often the driving force behind my arrogance and my addiction to stacking. I am the only person in IT that has been formally educated. I am sad that its true, "you must run twice as fast and jump twice as high." I think, *old folks were right.* I learn early on that in white spaces, I don't have the option to be both mediocre and black.

My ambition lands me a prominent teaching position among the same people I did grunt work with in IT. The same guys I started my old jobs many years before I arrived, are hooking up my computer and arranging my office. My old IT co-workers are in awe at my fearlessness. One guy joked to,

She went to the other side, I knew she was never one of us. I was not.

My teaching mentor is an older white woman who is the end all and be all of the computer science department. Dottie or Professor Barks, is the mother hen. As IT support, I remember supporting these instructors' computers for more than two years. None of them remember me.

Fear drives this space. The majority are beyond retirement age, and they work in technology, but they have no desire to learn anything new. They are threatened by anyone who challenges this notion. Of course, I challenge this notion, and because of this I do not fit in. I do dynamic work there, I teach six different types of computer courses, I am the only instructor who is credentialed to do this thanks to my master's degree I earned at a *for-profit* college a few years earlier.

To get this position, I send in an elaborate video production, with interviews from my references as opposed to just their names and numbers. I am what they call a *visiting scholar.* The scholar part refers to me and the visiting part means that I am temporary. I am ignored for two years and I don't know how to be seen without pushing. I turn to pot to ease the misalignment I feel in this environment. I don't know how to want to fit in and if I even should. They make it easy to disappear.

I sat in one meeting where the dean, a timid black man, solid beta male says, "Yasminah...what do you think?" I sit up straight and proud like the kid on the playground who is finally picked first for the dodgeball teams. I speak. I discuss social media, new course offerings that might bring in more students and a plethora of other modern technology related ideas. When I am done, the group sits quietly. The silence is loud. Loud like death metal. The energy in the room reaches an overwhelming level of stagnation. They look winded, as if just the thought of having to keep up with industry was enough to drive them to a nap. I sink. The dean seems interested, but he is also a guest in this white space, a figure head. He is not respected, relied upon or cherished; he knows this and so does everyone else.

Dottie steps in, "Yasminah, I think those are great ideas. We will consider each one." Dottie saves face, but I know I am being patronized. I despise being patronized. It feels small. And the fact that I can't address this without looking like a, God forbid, *angry black woman*, feels even smaller.

After this semester, I don't hear any word on whether I am to be the next permanent computer science instructor. It feels like I am a needle on a record player, when it's in the grooves, it makes beautiful music, but my time there feels more like a hip hop DJ scratching on the ones and twos at a Harlem block party. I feel lost, lost in a sea of mediocrity with no one to relate to. I miss Dr. Suleman, I miss feeling like I belong.

Dottie knocks on my office door one morning.

"Hi..." She looks solemn. I am on a call and she decides to wait. Dottie seems determined to have a moment with me.

"Hi..." I step outside of my office door to see where Dottie has tucked herself while I complete my call. She gazes at the floor, avoiding direct eye contact. Distant.

"I just want to tell you that the permanent position didn't come through." Crestfallen, she rambles on about budgets and the board of trustees. The air grows stale. "The others didn't want to tell you, but I thought that was a bad idea." Dottie added, fumfering her words.

I let her off the hook. Her face is bloodshot red. I wonder if they know I'm a pot head. I wonder if I received complaints. I wonder if this means I'm not good enough and I'm fooling myself. I wonder for those short moments, then I feel relaxed. Relief. I feel the sweet relief of heading into the direction of myself. I don't know where this is, but I know that letting go of this rich but expired opportunity with ease is a necessary step in that direction.

"It's okay," I add... "I wasn't sure if this is what..." Dottie interrupts me. "If you need anything, just let me know." She darts away. I attempt to stack but I am not allowed my, *I didn't want it anyway,* response. It would have been a lie. Even though I'm not sure this is my destiny, I still want the opportunity to give all I have. This is the same way I feel about Danny. By taking me out of his life, I'm not allowed to give any of myself. With no direction, my anxiety rushes in like a ghost; in the still of the night, filling every inch of my insides, a cloud of dark energy. I question my ability to be wanted. I need answers and they are not visible. My answer for now is just more pot. I don't have another way to cope.

JAMEELAH RAOOF

CHAPTER THIRTEEN

Stacking

I began my journey of stacking before I even knew it was a part of me. The more frequently life called for me to enter white spaces, the better I became at talking about what I *have* as opposed to who I *am*. I mostly stack with the conversations I choose to have with my daughters when we're running errands. If someone is walking down the aisle, I am compelled to bring up something we are proud of that would make us look a little bit more than typical. I say, *oh look pumpkin, those are like the shades I had on our vacation to San Diego,* or I say, *we better hurry if we don't want to be late to ballet class,* and most recently, *remind me to sign you two up for ski school before we get to Pagosa Springs.* And on and on. I make these comments just loud enough to be heard but just intimately enough to seem genuine. I feel better when I stack, the performativity of this act is satisfying for me, whether anyone around us is paying attention or not.

My earliest memories of intentionally stacking was when I worked at the Galleria mall in North Dallas at Ann Taylor. One lazy week day afternoon there is a black woman perusing the clearance racks towards the back of the store. She came in the store with a few shopping bags in her hands. Commission-wise, we didn't make any money off clearance items, so when customers walked in and jetted straight to the back of the store for those racks, we generally didn't follow. This store has maybe one black woman customer per week. Diversity is almost non-existent. A week earlier there was a meeting for employees about theft. The numbers were reportedly high. The largest area of stolen goods had consistently been in hosiery. In this store, the hosiery rack is placed in the fitting room. My common sense tells me that when those little old white ladies go to the back they are obviously stealing stockings. I look around and no one acknowledges this. *Do they truly believe that little old white ladies don't steal?* I think.

This afternoon, the customer, who happens to be a black woman, had been trying on clothes over her own clothing in the mirror near the clearance racks. I am the only person on the sales floor. The manager comes out and notices the woman. Her eyes bug out. She finds me and exclaims, "You should be watching her!" She reminds me of the recent stolen goods meeting and how we should all be on high alert. In this moment, I have to step outside of myself. Since I have always dismissed race, it takes me a while to figure out that the manager wants me to watch this woman because she is black. I don't know how to take this. I could be the good negro and hound a customer who does not need my help, or I could ask why. I went with the latter.

The manager then explained to me that "women like her", don't usually shop in this store, so when they do come in we need to pay close attention to them. I then say, "precisely, if we rarely get black customers and the theft issue is through the roof because of our existing customers, old white ladies, shouldn't I watch them more closely?" She huffed off, cheeks red, pretending to be helpful to the woman until she becomes annoyed and leaves the store.

The most interesting thing about this scenario is that the manager still never sees anything wrong with deciding that black women are thieves and that this is just a fact. This tainted me. I began to look at all the white women I work with differently. I wondered what they thought of me. I wondered if they only saw me as black.

I notice that many of the women I work with at Ann Taylor are seeking college degrees but are having a hard time finishing because of the demands of the job. I have two college degrees, I purposely make mention of them in just about every conversation that is started with me. I want them to feel as small as the cube they've put me and every other black woman in. I want them to feel limited. I want them to feel trapped. I want them to feel miniscule in their own white space, like an *other.*

This attitude becomes a habit, which over time becomes a significant aspect of my belief system. Mediocrity scares me. To leave this life and be no better than the average Joe is downright suffocating to me. Some days, the only thing I can think about is how to be better than the fray. How to avoid being boxed in and how to make sure other people know how great I am. Quietly of course.

I remember during my marriage, my ex and I were having a serious argument and I kept shouting out, "I'm better than you! I'm better than you!" I have no idea why it was so important to be better. This seemingly shallow ideology is what I have been stuck with as far back as I can remember. The therapist was right about me having fishbowl mentality. I want people to see me as flawless as unreal and unattainable. This is lonely, but right now I prefer solitude over mediocrity. Stacking is my religion.

CHAPTER FOURTEEN

Romantic Loser

Nearly a month has passed and still no word from Danny. I begin to see it as an auspicious journey that has come to an end. Besides, there is no future for a crass, self-proclaimed *hick* in my life. He will not bring me prosperity or major success. He is not that kind of white. I sit perched on my bed with one dim lamp glowing. My pipe on one side and my phone on the other. Being high doesn't even feel high any more. When I smoke I'm not lifted and giggly and these days, I rarely get the munchies. It is strictly here to stave off anxiety; that persistent *bitch* who is the bane of my existence.

I stare pragmatically over at my romantic vison board. I puff a few times, trying to inhale deeper than usual. Making deliberate effort to reach all the nooks and crannies of my lungs, hoping that might offer a deeper effect. I read somewhere that marijuana works better the deeper it reaches into your lunges. I don't feel any different. I refuse to move away from regular weed, which my pot dealer affectionately refers to as *reggie*. I need to function. I need to raise my daughters and I need to be as clear as possible.

My romantic vision board had been created soon after I returned from Puerto Rico with Rogelio. I demanded that he tell me whether he wanted me for good or not and he never calls again. I'm so pissed after him because I broke so many rules simply because no matter what I said, at my core, I did not believe I could do better. In every other part of my life, career, academics, being a mother, yoga; better comes fairly easy to me.

Romantically, *better* alludes me. I feel like a romantic loser. I say don't want to want a relationship, but the truth is, I do. I'm angry about romance. I am angry that in my circle none of the women are happily married, or the men, for that matter. I am angry that I feel as though I come from a tribe of loners, narcissists who only care about their own needs in relationships and never consider that the other person is indeed, a real person. I am angry that the men I date are judged so heavily by others who wouldn't know a great relationship if it smacked them upside their head. I am angry that even with all of these inconsistencies, I still care about people's opinions.

So many opinions, I often feel smothered, choked, and bludgeoned by social rules, decapitated by expectations. I want to be free. Danny is my chance to be free. My chance to ignore what might not work and to nurture what might. But I look at my vision board and all I hear are whispers, chatter, gossip, judgement; they echo about in the recesses of my brain and become tangible through worry, fear, and doubt; which is the next-door neighbor of anxiety and anxiety unresolved turns into *dis-ease*, either mentally or physically. I don't want to be sick.

I don't want to be compared to other women because we wear the same size clothing. I don't want to be at odds with people in my life because they lack appropriate boundaries. I don't want to take myself too seriously. I want to be free. I feel I will never have the romance I desire unless I learn to untether myself from these mental clutches, clutches most are not aware are anchored so deep within me.

My vision board stares back at me. The burnt marijuana leaves create a haze, matching the haze I feel when contemplating Love. I reach over to grab a sip of my bottled water. My eyes catch a glimpse of the clippers I used to cut Danny's hair. I hop up and bury them in the drawer. I don't need a reminder of being abandoned twice by a man I don't even see a future with.

Stick to your standards! Great men are still out there! Fear not...the dating pool is infinite! My vison board screams at me. My actions don't reflect belief or trust in these truths sprawled across my board and I can't understand why. I add white men to my infinite dating pool and to my chagrin, it proves to be more of the same.

~

Upward facing dog, downward facing dog, raise your right leg up, inhale, step it through, exhale, warrior one, inhale, move through your vinyasa flow, exhale, chaturanga arms, inhale, upward facing dog... Yoga is my solace. In this space I am whole, I am in a trance, a moving meditation. I don't have time to think. Just breathe and move, move and breathe. My body is the strongest it's ever been. My arms are cut and defined, my ass looks like two perfect cantaloupes and my abs are visible without effort. I feel happy. I feel happy that I have something, something I'm good at and something that makes me better. Something I'm good at that cannot be attributed to anyone. No one can take credit for my yoga, yoga is mine. My body flowing rhythmically with my breath feels like an ocean view, it feels the way seeing the ocean dance feels. Its hypnotic. There is no anxiety in my practice. There is no room for fear, only room for action. Fear and worry are the ugly step sisters that must take a back seat when

Cinderella is ready to shine. Yoga is my Cinderella. She dances with or without the prince.

I tune out my mental jargon and catch a snippet of what the instructor is saying. "If you have a muscle that you can't seem to get to act right, maybe instead of stretching it, you need to strengthen it first." I think, *could romance be my stubborn muscle? Have I been stretching it to no avail? Does It need to be nourished and strengthened before I stretch it again?* I ponder. I continue to flow, feeling like a major golden nugget of wisdom has just been dropped onto my path. This nugget is so heavy and so awkward, do I pick it up or do I do what's easy and leave it there?

It's been six weeks since I'd heard from Danny. One quiet afternoon, I sit on the couch reading a book about how to identify clearly what I want from a relationship. Reading line after line I feel so fatigued. I feel I'm at the bottom of a mountain having to hike through treacherous weather, packs of wolves and venomous snakes in order to reach the summit. The summit is where life is, its where love is. The view is beautiful there, I hear. I no longer want to talk about it, I am ready to receive it. I am ready to conquer this journey on my own. The phone rings, its Danny's number. I have only two reasons why I will take his call. First, I want to make sure he is okay and second, I want to know what his unconventional presence means in my life.

I slide the little arrow on the face of my smartphone towards the green symbol and not the red. "Hello..." I answer flatly.

"Hey girl...its Danny..." His tone is bright, light and chipper.

I pause, he waits for me to indicate what his call means to me. He dips only his toe into my space to see if my energy is gentle and warm or ice cold.

"I been meaning to call you..." He fills the quiet space before it grows too large and too heavy.

"Oh...okay..." I fain aloofness. There is only a thin, rickety door between that enormous, awkward, and painfully empty space growing between our words and Danny is manning the door. Each time the door tries to swing open, he's leaning his whole body on it, pushing back against that space.

"I mean...I was going to call you but I didn't know if you wanted to talk to me. I thought, well she hasn't called me either, maybe she doesn't want to talk?" Danny rambles out a response that attempts to equate our actions as they pertain to one another.

"Hmmm...last time we talked you said you would call me." I am direct. He is not accustomed to a woman being direct with him without being emotionally charged.

The space opens, this time he does not resist. He realizes the awkward conversation about his disappearance must fully manifest before moving onto pleasantries.

"Well..." He scatters. "That's true but I thought you would call too."

I hold the phone. I don't give him an out. I don't help him lie.

"My bad...I know I should have called...my bad...I apologize for that." Danny concedes.

"How's the healing going?" I feel we have bumbled around long enough. I'm not mad at him. I'm not sure how I feel. I'm just on the other end of the phone and present.

"I'm doing great, I should be back at work by the end of the month." Danny replies. He then alludes to wanting us to hang out again.

My mouth says yes but my insides recoil a bit. I know that he is okay, and after all, that is all I wanted. I don't trust myself. I was born into a world of right and wrong answers. I lie about my insides to make those on the outside more comfortable. This method of lying about my insides work. Others accept me, and because of this acceptance, I am tolerable to myself.

Danny plans a date for us to go to a rock concert at a bar on the weekend. He says blue jeans are okay. I don't normally wear jeans, but I say, "okay."

I let Danny pick me up. He shows up to my home in his mother's suv. He goes on about his beautiful white Volkswagen that needs a new motor. In essence, his car is in the shop, and has been since I met him. Danny says his old Saturn hatchback is not nice enough to take me out in. His railroad job is dirty, and this dirt finds a permanent home in his little Saturn.

This time, I let him step into my home. I'm not ready to leave yet so I show him to the couch. He tries not to look around, as so many do. Once I leave the room, he will evaluate me through my space, through my belongings, freely, without my presence creating self-consciousness. Danny looks much better. He is limping a bit and one arm is hanging from his body not as relaxed as the other. His hand on that arm seems lifeless, without energy or sensation. He avoids using it. I pretend I don't notice.

It is four in the afternoon when we arrive at the Irish pub for the concert. There are no windows, just two large metal doors. The parking lot is full, but it's hard to know if the vehicles present are customers of the bar or customers of the other shops in the small strip. I want as much data as possible uploaded to my brain about this place before I go in. Danny opens one of the big metal doors for me. If darkness were like light, it would have poured out of the door and onto the sidewalk. But darkness doesn't pour. Darkness is nothing without light. Shadows would have no life without light. It is dark in the bar, but not dark enough for my black skin to go unseen.

The woman at the door is quietly taken aback by me and Danny's presence. She names the price, Danny takes out his wallet and we find an intimate spot. I feel like we have just walked onto the set of, *Son's of Anarchy.* This bar is grungy. The women look tired and the men look worn. This white space is not better. It is rough. Danny has already paid so we sit. He is in foreign territory too. The only thing he has in common with these people is skin color. Danny is not a biker, is not into tattoos and does not indulge in death metal. Death metal plays steadily in background before the bands are ready. There is a heavy layer of bleakness resting upon every surface and every patron. Danny scopes out the place, orders himself some food and tries not to show discomfort.

"I bet everyone in here is holding." Danny leans over and whispers to me. I chuckle. The dormant playful energy between us awakens.

"Is this Sons of Anarchy or what?" I laugh. I have never experienced such a sharp culture shock. I don't want to pretend to fit in. I want to observe this environment. I hone in on the very spirit of it. I watch them watch us.

The first band plays more death metal. This display of musical butchering does not impress Danny. We snicker at each other. Danny is country and this, to him, is not music. We have this in common.

Our presence feels like a coveted portrait painted centuries earlier, stolen from forbidden lands that beckon the recognizing of our racially divided past and our denial of our racially divided present. We awaken both disdain and puzzlement.

CHAPTER FIFTEEN

White Thanksgiving

I contemplate Thanksgiving in the same way I contemplate love. *What is this heaviness of the holidays? What does it mean to bring someone home? Does it mean you love them or does it simply mean you find joy in their company and you don't mind your family meeting this person? Do I construct my own meaning of Thanksgiving or do I use the construct already provided for me? Does this negate the fact that I don't believe in the predetermined construct?* Confusing, I know. I am confused. Unlike Love, I don't see what I stand to gain from the holiday dog and pony show.

Danny is the not the *bring me home to your parents,* kind of guy. In my assessment, through all the romantic comedies I have consumed since my teen years, I am sure Danny is the complete opposite of the *bring me home to your parents,* kind of guy. I decide that if Danny will be there, I will have the dinner at my home. On my turf, I control the narrative. My home all by itself stacks me higher than any deficit Danny's presence might add. I own my own home and the safe space I've cultivated within it.

The holiday arrives and there is much talk about whether or not I will visit Danny's family. Women generally internalize the holidays as a time to be claimed, to be acknowledged, to perform the role of girlfriend or significant other. I feel none of this with Danny. I just want to make it through, around and over. I just want to, want to want this. To want to be exotic enough to have a non-black boyfriend, to be the kind of woman who is too busy being magnificent to be concerned with race. I want to be seen as the kind of woman that transcends tradition and cultural expectations. Unruled and unapologetic.

I thirst for expansion and Danny represents expansion. This is what I think the women who date and marry white men think. They long for something different, and this sets them apart. They thumb their noses at those who call them sellouts, they thumb their noses at tradition and expectation; they thumb their noses at carrying the wounds of American slavery as a badge of honor or a trope of victimhood. They make their own rules and the man on their arm is an external manifestation of *I don't give a f*ck what you think*. Or in my case, I don't *want* to give a f*ck what you think.

This is different from black men dating white women. They are not seen as heroic rule breakers but instead conformists, sheeples that lust after white flesh and deny black women the right to be a wife. They are charged with leaving black women stranded on a desert island of singleness and single-motherness from where there is no escape by means of tradition and expectation. I escape, Danny is my ship to the mainland where the chosen women reside. A pirate ship maybe, but a ship nonetheless.

I convince Danny that I am looking forward to Thanksgiving with his family. He plans to visit his cousins in a small town, forty miles east of Dallas. They celebrate the day before to be sure that everyone can attend. Forty miles is long. Forty miles east of all traces of diversity. I am nervous. I puff a lot early in the morning on this day, more than usual. My insides began to take on familiar feelings of angst. Like a volcanic mountain on the verge of an upsurge. My reservations are like magma attempting to find its way to the top and my pot acts like a formidable plug, allowing only a drivel of lava to escape in the form of brief crying spells and sudden surges of anger. I want out of this day.

Danny tells me his cousins and other family members are through-and-through racists, "but they're okay," he says. "They don't act on it." I remember he said the same of Gail, his mother. Danny says this as if their lack of racist acts, make the effects of stealth racism any less consequential. As if by employing only stealth racism they do not enable the avenues through which tangible racism languishes.

Danny is aggressively honest and happily unfiltered. He tells me that I don't act like a black girl at least once every few days. My Mexican friend said her husband once called her a coconut and accompanied by her revelation was a soft giggle. She thought it was cute. Coconut means brown on the outside and white within. As if the word coconut, which boils her rich Mexican heritage down to essentially pointing out the absence of stereotypical *cholo* catch phrases, clothing and mannerisms, is somehow a compliment.

When she mentions this to me, I feel compelled to tell her that I had been similarly referred to as an *oreo*. I giggle too. I don't know why I find this amusing, but inside, I know that the absence of what makes me different signifies the presence of acceptance. I think, *you can relax around me, my insides will make you comfortable with my outside.* Even though acceptance of these terms feels like an apology for being black, to Danny *oreo* also means that I am *better.* Our giggle is the chuckle of *better* women, taking a quiet moment to acknowledge their betterness, in the safe space that resides within the irrational boundaries of our mostly concealed xenocentrism. For better or worse, I am considered one of the good blacks and not a threat. And she is seen as barely Mexican.

It's the afternoon before Thanksgiving, Danny picks me up sharply at 3:00 pm. I wear a short cobalt blue dress, a wool silk blend. The dress is printed with an art deco likeness. I wear cobalt blue tights and chocolate brown cowboy boots. I choose this outfit because, no matter where I have been in it, I am stopped and fawned over. Beauty is my secret weapon. In my mind I picture his family to be fairly mediocre with many of the matriarchs being overweight. White spaces refer to skinny as beautiful. Skinny and beautiful go hand in hand. My body makes women who are not slim self-conscious. I don't agree with this reaction, but I am aware of it. To me my body is just the wrapper. My svelteness pleases others and when it pleases others, it pleases me. In white spaces, you are praised heavily, for being skinny. I am skinny. Toned but skinny. In black spaces, you are not praised for this. This is quite conflicting for an upwardly mobile black woman. Fit does not mean skinny in the world I come from, it means ample butt and hips, small waist, thick thighs, flat stomach, and breasts, well, breasts are rarely discussed.

In white spaces, women envy you depending on how skinny you are. They want to befriend you more and they watch you from afar. Thin mostly beats race. The women that might not approach you because you're black, might feel compelled if you're skinny. These spaces are obsessed with thin. A big black woman is definitely out of place; unless her demeanor is apologetic and humble, and she doesn't take up too much space. This kind of black woman is endearing and everyone wants to hug her, and calm her fears that she is not accepted. But a big, black, confident woman, well, she is supernatural. In white spaces they wonder, *how can she be so confident and so big?* White spaces are infinitely intrigued by the big, beautiful, confident, black woman.

Tim is with Danny today. Like most pre-teens, he has come to the moment in his journey where he is not easily impressed by his father. Danny's mere presence is a nuisance to him, which Tim shields in an attempt to prolong their harmony. Danny comes up with all sorts of explanations for why Tim prefers to spend time with his mother; she cooks better, their house is cozier, his friends all live near her, etc. Through our conversation, it's become clear that Danny is the black sheep of the family, the wild card, the source of gossip, excitement and heartache. If any man in his family would bring a black girl to Thanksgiving dinner, it would be Danny.

If the stunned faces of the parents at Tim's baseball game I attended for a few moments one Saturday afternoon was any indication of what I was walking into, the day would be long; in slow motion and every bit of the uneasiness would be felt, absorbed and relived on a loop, in real time as the moments continue to unfold.

Surely Gail had mentioned my possible attendance to members of their family. I am hoping she did. On the long-ride there, I where my blackness like the Scarlett Letter A, but instead a letter B, a heavy B. I prepare my demure disposition. I try to remember the lines from my self-help books that tell me I am more than my appearance, that I can't let others define me. I know this intellectually but my insides, my vulnerable bits, they reside somewhere else. They reside on the fringe of self-love and self-loathe. *How can I love myself wholly when the space I occupy, the white spaces that dominate prosperity, require me to reject pieces of myself at the pleasure of the crowd I am submerged in?* This sucks.

I stare blankly out of the window. Danny plays his usual country music. Tim is consumed by a smart phone that he treats more like an appendage than a device. I am never sure if Tim is actually using his phone in a meaningful way or if he uses it as a buffer to engage his surroundings without actually actively engaging. Sort of like, *I'm here when it's convenient, and I'm not here when it's not.*

I don't puff right before we leave today. As much as I love to self-medicate, I know that pot has its limitations. It can only relax me so much without affecting the disposition of my face. I can't risk rose colored eyes, blanking out in the middle of conversations or the slight smell that often lingers on my tongue. These people have no close connections with blacks and for better or worse, to them I represent all black women they know. My secret goal for this day is to stun with my svelteness, charm with my demureness and snub with my intellect.

"You okay over there, girl?" Danny reaches for the volume on the stereo. It's quiet enough to hear Tim's video game.

Danny's eyes sparkle like blue marbles in the dimming sunlight. Briefly, I recall how different we are. How different his values are, how different our families are, how opposite we just are.

"I'm fine," I snap out of my thick fog. A fog mostly due to the three Xanax I popped before Danny arrived.

Danny flashes a smile at me. A smile that in the past, it's clear, has gotten him both into and out of trouble. Danny played high school football, he dated cheerleaders, was voted most valuable player and had been king of prom. He is a legend in his own right, with more than a few high school crushes that follow him on Facebook and *like* and comment on all his pictures. He never ventures too far from the small town that coddles him. They see Danny as the hometown hero, bad boy, that ultimately *made it,* without having to change or leave everyone behind.

Danny's hand is still not fully operable. Two of his fingers sustained such severe nerve damage that four surgeries have not been able to restore their function. Danny grunts about his fingers often, always ending his short rant with a less than cheerful, "It is what it is."

After a nearly forty-five-minute drive through the wide-open landscapes that fall squarely between a series of small interstate towns, we finally arrive at his cousin's house. I feel as though I signed up for a skydiving class and the experience is becoming surreal. I know I'm going to jump out of the plane, but the actuality of the moment takes on a whole new meaning. I am about to be the first black person to step into these people's home. I know this because Danny said I would be. He also tells me that if anyone says anything off-colored to me because I'm black, he will kick their ass. I like that he likes to protect me, but I am also a little disappointed that he feels these words must even be spoken.

We pull up to a winding street that leads to his cousins residence. The sun is now orange and subdued. The glow turns the nearby field of tall country grass into golden stalks, gently coifed by an ever-present zephyr.

The road is named after Danny's family. Over the horizon appears a massive property. The home is so massive that I doubt that this is where we are headed. Danny says nothing at first, as if the size of the home had not registered since he is still pouring his attention into the GPSs' instructions.

"Damn!" Danny shouts. He is overt in his observations.

"Shit his house is big!" Danny adds. In the rearview mirror Tim says nothing and barely raises his eyes away from his smartphone.

"It's beautiful." I whisper, mostly to myself. "Is all of this his land?" I ask. I fully indulge my child-like wonder before we exit the car. I don't have the luxury of acting too giddy about the home. My nonchalant demeanor will show either I am familiar with this level of wealth or that I possess a level of self-control that does not expose my internal reaction. Either way, I feel these are my choices.

As we get closer, I see that the three-car garage is open and furnished with several rows of banquet style tables and chairs. I think, *Shit...there's a lot of people here.* Suddenly my brown skin is all I can think about. I want to hide, to run, to step into some white skin if only for a minute; and then after I've met everyone, my white skin would slowly transform back into its native brown hue. So slowly that no one would notice. I feel like I am whacking them upside their heads with my brown skin, pouring out of Danny's car and pouring into their white space, without relent.

I hate this shit. I hate that I am considering snapping into the "good negro" routine. Contemplating ways to make sure they are comfortable with me bombards my thoughts. I hate feeling like I have something to prove even when the proving is easy. I hate that people I don't even know possess the ability to make me feel so small and so wrong. I don't share this discomfort with anyone. I lie with my smile.

Danny is a natural leader. His white-maleness allows him to default to this position without thought or provocation. I follow behind him and Tim follows behind me. Danny is wearing a seemingly out of date club going shirt made out of velour, in a blend of soft grays. Eminem's *Lose Yourself* comes to mind. *I'm a champion and I'm better than this...I'm so much better than this,* I think. I ponder if I date Danny to face this fear head on. To face my fear of feeling small in white spaces. It pisses me off and I'm tired of feeling pissed off.

Their home is full. A huge "NOBAMA" sign hangs in the garage adjacent to a small but consuming confederate flag. I inhale deeply. My Xanax is working. My insides are calm, but my mind is on auto-repeat. These people are not working-class, or lower-class, they are upper-middle class and their home is jaw-dropping. I think about Chris Rock saying that him and Mary J. Blige are the only black people in his neighborhood and how his neighbors are dentists and professors. I don't know any upper-middle class black people with a home like this. In my own neighborhood, my neighbors are working class, company people. I am by far the most educated on the block with two advanced degrees and two undergraduate degrees. If hard work is the only definer of worthiness for a lifestyle like this, then I more than fit the bill.

I realize a painful truth I have ignored with ease or possibly out of self-preservation; race does matter, access does matter, networks do matter; now and generationally.

Networks are subjected to racism. Networks are subjected to classism and classism is the first cousin of race. In America, anyway. It's a vicious circle. A circle whose entry has been purposefully denied to me and generations of people that look just like me. I feel foolish. I feel foolish without a real rhyme or reason for it. I don't know how Danny's cousin acquired this land and this house but suddenly I feel nothing I can say, stack or do, will make me feel any better. I sense a strange irrational feeling of *them* winning, of whites winning. I feel blacks and whites in America are always in a fierce spiritual rivalry and I am not winning this round for my people. I never consider anyone to be *my people* except for my family of origin. But now, in a matter of seconds, I feel deeply connected to black American people; to their stories, and both their pain and their triumphs.

It's not about the house but instead about the feeling of white privilege in white spaces, their abundance always seems ill-gotten. I think, *you are no better than me, but you feel as though you deserve this more than me, just because.* Just because I am a daughter of the oppressed and you are the children of the oppressor? I hate that I feel I need to consider what they consider me to be. I pull my thoughts together to greet Gail. I smile.

"Hi Yasminah," Gail says standing in the kitchen, organizing the food in a buffet style. Tim is already gone, lost in the crowd of family, his sea of sameness. It's happening, the facial expressions of shock follow us through the house as Danny introduces me as his girlfriend. We knock the wind out of the room. The home is a blur of custom-made cowboy boots, shiny belt buckles, big hair and expensive furnishings. And high-end turquoise costume jewelry, lots of turquoise costume jewelry. Hearing Danny say girlfriend feels strange. It's like when you take two south poles of a magnet and try vigorously to push them together, but they won't attract, they don't even like each other. The title *girlfriend* does not agree with me. I don't know how to be one and each time he says it, I feel more and more like a fraud, like a journalist that has infiltrated the enemy by befriending one of their own.

I think back to late one night after talking on the phone for a bit, Danny rambling and me, high, but listening; he effectuated our budding romance.

"Hey..." Danny stopped in the middle of our conversation. His words trailed off into space.

"I know we got off to a bumpy start, but you stuck with me through all of it..." His words trailed off again. I think that it wasn't that hard to stick with him because I am not in love and don't foresee Danny being my *one*. I replied with an attentive, "mmhmm."

"I want you to be my girlfriend, meaning I don't want to be seeing anybody else..." This time his voice does not trail off and he is direct. I sit briefly. I feel almost obligated to say yes out of my sense of adventure. Because he is white, a different kind of white than I'm used to. I had never been asked to be someone's girl so directly and without any level of mystique or confusion. The mere chivalry of his gesture, to the adventurer in me, required a yes.

I smile at Gail, at least I think I do. This ride is moving too fast to keep up. Three other women in the kitchen completely ignore our presence. "I don't care who has a problem with us, I'm still going to Thanksgiving and they better not say nothing..." Danny said days earlier. Thinking of Danny's declaration softens the hard space these women create. And that my skin creates.

We tour the entire home on our own. I am in the thick of it. Danny and I eventually land on one of the couches near the fireplace.

The rattle of disbelief is still lingering in each small gathering throughout the house, even the children seem to believe they are seeing a ghost. Children don't hide or pretend, they stare willfully and with no grand purpose or set stopping point. They aren't quite sure what's wrong with the picture, but they know something is out of place. They feel it. The adults radiate it.

I sit quietly as Danny chats with different people about his accident. I'm poised like a debutant, on the rustic, leather sofa, my legs crossed, and fingers interlocked, wrapping around my highest knee. Danny's eyes find me but that's all, it's no covert communication of our needs from across the room, that only he and I might understand. We are not connected in that way. For me, our connection feels shallow, but on his end, this is more than enough.

The whole room feels shallow, especially during the group prayer that breaks out in the middle of the large gathering space. Danny's cousin thanks everyone for coming out. They all hold hands around the room and bow their heads. I think, *Are white people spiritual...this feels odd?* Danny's cousin bows his head and barks out a prayer. He sounds eerily similar to Jimmy Swaggart. The praise goes on for what feels like half an hour but is really more like five minutes. Danny fidgets and tries his best not to acknowledge this massive praise session. I can see that prayer is foreign to Danny. He once told me that he didn't believe in God and that he conducted his life accordingly.

"You ready to eat something?" Danny speaks in his inside voice. I nudge him and gesture my attention back to the prayer. He begins to gnaw at his finger nails, which are already bitten to the quick. I like seeing this side of him, it is raw and untamed and unamused by expectations or decorum.

It's not like any of the bible thumpers look up to see where the noise is coming from. They are in deep praise, at least it appears they are. I had been raised to believe that most whites were cold and unfeeling, after all, my parents would say, "these people are the descendants of those who pillaged and destroyed the Indians and the same who put Japanese in concentration camps and the same who enslaved Africans for hundreds of years...you can't trust people like that." This is what I like about Danny, his personality doesn't require me to adjust the *truths* I hold about whites, no matter how absurd. He is mostly ignorant to all things black and at times, I find this amusing.

We eat and the food tastes as bland as it looks. For me, this is not a white thing. I am from New Orleans and white people there can cook.

Danny and I sit at one of the long tables in the garage. Someone planned this setup with great care. Tim is nowhere to be found. My Xanax is wearing off, but I do feel better. The screaming stomach aches that usually mars me with pain and renders me immobile are subtle. Subtle enough for me to pick at the mostly beige colored plate of food that sits before me. Danny inhales his food as he discusses what we'll do after we leave. I like that Danny doesn't have a ton of patience for large family gatherings. He has more patience for crowds that he can sink into anonymously, crowds that do not have a story about him and who they know him to be. I watch Gail put on another persona, a polite and cautious demeanor. It is clear that this is the side of the family she wants to impress, knowingly or unknowingly she seems to be stacking a bit herself.

Absolutely no one has spoken to us. They are all cordial and smiling with one another, but they say nothing to me when I sit alone and nothing to us when Danny and I are together. The isolation is clear, but strangely, I'm okay with it. I like to know where I stand with people, even if it means standing alone.

I believe I struggle with the validity of race as a motivating factor for hatred and inequality because I was raised as an "other" amongst *others*. An "insider within". My parents weren't the type of black folks who deemed it useful to imitate whites in order to make them more comfortable. My childhood was not about white people, it wasn't about what they did or did not *allow* us to do. My childhood was explicitly and unequivocally about us, my mother's children being excellent for the sake of excellence. The "white man" only came up in philosophical conversations about how he had devil tendencies and how much better us black folks were than them. I did not live in poverty nor see poverty on a daily basis. The whites I grew up around were just as pay check to pay check as the blacks I lived around.

We lived in an all-black suburban neighborhood until I was five-years-old. The type of neighborhood where black families were intact, where everyone owned their homes, where fathers were riding bikes with their children after school, where lawns were mowed every Saturday morning and where skating as a family in the street before dark was common. As an adult, when I look back, it is clear when crack cocaine had been introduced, adopted and embedded in black communities. Our home was robbed twice that I remember. My parents then moved us into a quiet neighborhood on the "white side" of town. My mother fell in love with the large two-bedroom home, sitting on a full acre of land with a five- car carport and a back house complete with a stage, bathroom and dance floor. In years to come, my parents would add on three more bedrooms, making our home the largest in the neighborhood. My parents didn't succeed to catch up to white folks, they succeeded because they enjoyed success.

They had no doubt that they could surpass whites, and they always did.

I had never experienced a world where it was the norm to salivate after white privilege or to see white beauty as the only viable expression of beauty. Blackness was taught as something to be proud of and not the bane of one's existence. The community of blackness I had been nurtured in relied on self-education as a tool to disregard the "white man's" systems and make a life and business for yourself. I could not relate to black or white counterparts at school because my parents were disconnected from the mediocrity that bore whiteness as though it were the crème de la crème. They saw through everything. The N word was a bad word, never used in any fashion or form as a term of endearment. I still cringe when I hear that word casually used by friends, musicians or in movies. My siblings and I watched documentaries about Africa, Civil Rights and even the animal kingdom for sport. The television only came on with my parents' permission. It was understood that we could only watch PBS and ironically enough, The Cosby Show. Organic food was just our way of life, it was not special, and it was definitely not reserved for the white elite. They did not teach hate, submission, or fear, they taught intellectual superiority. While they were no longer card-carrying members of the Nation of Islam, the remnants of their unconventional education lingered. They showed no interest in being the *good black*.

JAMEELAH RAOOF

CHAPTER SIXTEEN

Black Thanksgiving

Thanksgiving at my home and with my family is on Thanksgiving Day. My home is buzzing with preparation. My family would never trust me with the task of baking a turkey or making the gumbo. I have not proven myself to that degree. They know I can cook but making a turkey and making the gumbo are two tasks reserved for the seasoned cooks. I make vegetables and bake a whole chicken that I stuff with large chunks of white onion and fresh orange slices.

I am always reaching for something outside of my norm, and with lots of resistance, each year I try to bring some of that to my family. Like the time I brought homemade pizza to a family event, or that one gettogether where I tried light snacks and wine instead of a large dinner. The complaints crawled around the house like termites gobbling up wood. My family is from New Orleans, if it doesn't contain seafood, rice or more rice, it's not the kind of meal they're interested in.

Danny promises to bring the potato salad. He says his mother makes the best potato salad in the world. This is how Danny speaks about himself and anything he is proud of, in hyperboles. It is common in black culture that a big deal is made out of who made the potato salad. It is a special dish that requires an involved process and black folks often say, "I don't eat just anybody potato salad." I know my sisters will cringe when they hear that we will get second hand potato salad, made by Gail, a woman whom I explained on different occasions might be a racist.

My mother seems to be less concerned about her racism and more concerned about whether or not Gail has pets, she says, "You know how white folks are with their pets, they let the cats walk aross the kitchen counter and the dogs eat off their plates." I have heard this so many times throughout the years that I'm not the slightest bit surprised when this is her exact reaction. The funniest part is that she knows how often she repeats this. I picture the way her nose turns up as if inside pets were the worst decision anyone could make in their life. Forget racism, *are they those pet people?*

My guests arrive an hour late. This is common. We set the time earlier than we want everyone to show up and voila, everyone arrives at the perfect time. Danny is punctual. He and Tim sit with anticipation on the sofa.

"Where is everybody?" He grumbles rhetorically while flipping through options on Netflix. Tim's face is buried deep into his smartphone.

"This is disrespectful!" Danny says. He fidgets.

"Where I'm from, if you set a time for an event to start, that's what time everybody should show up." He looks to me for confirmation that his feelings are valid.

I think, *maybe colored people time is a real thing?* Often affectionately referred to as "cp" time in black spaces. I'm forced to consider blackness once again.

"Does it matter? At least I'm ready and we know everyone is coming, its

Thanksgiving." I holler back from the kitchen towards the den.

Danny voices his discontentment with my less than punctual family and friends every five minutes until the first guest arrives. Lateness has a domino effect, once the first guest shows, the others are always shortly behind. Danny's need to tell everyone who arrives that they are late is rattling my nerves. I retreat to my bedroom bathroom and puff a few times near the window. I need to be in that empty space that pot provides. I need to be emptied of my cares. The smoke pushes my worries to a safe space inside of me that makes them hard to access.

Danny prances through my home like a peacock, as if he pays the mortgage. From one end of the room I watch my brother size him up at the other end of the room. He wants to see what it is I see in Danny. My brother believes me to be special, so he is searching for the specialness in Danny.

However, Danny's specialness only resides in our odd pairing, alone and in his natural habitat, he is not very special at all.

Danny promised his mother after his accident he wouldn't drink anymore. He did well for a while. A non-drinking Danny is a subdued Danny. I knew he would drink again simply because I know addictions. I know that If you don't decide on your own terms, you will revert back to what works. My ex would attempt to get me to stop smoking pot by hiding it when he went to work, which only made me want it more. So much more that when I found it and used it, I would say nothing and stash a little for later. I hoped my absence of discussing it would convince my ex that it was no longer an issue.

I despise drinking. I think drinking is sloppy and lends itself to the glorification of lacking self-control. Pot on the other hand, does not influence my self-control, at least not the regular weed I smoke. In my mind, drinkers are loud and kill people on the road. They are irresponsible with the feelings of others once they get few drinks in them and when the night is over, they claim a narcissistic innocence to all the garbage they allowed to slip through their lips, all runny and messy like diarrhea because...well...they were drinking.

Danny is a legit drinker. I know that I am giving him a pass because for now, I enjoy the exoticness of our pairing, more than I hate that he is a drinker.

Tim finds the company of a few of my male cousins who are all of similar ages. They play video games in my guest room. I think, *I wonder how Tim feels about being around so many black folks.* It's different being a minority when you're used to being the majority. In New Orleans blacks are the majority just about everywhere you go. Dallas is different that way.

My family of origin and extended family are all quite welcoming to Danny. In passing, I hear him more than once tell a guest that he has a black son. Danny doesn't say that the boy is the son of his older cousin who tends to date black men with problems. Or should I say, men with problems, who happen to be black. And of course, this is the only interaction his family has with a black man on personal level; a loser who loves drugs more than his family and who doesn't visit or take care of his kids. I think, *why do some white women seem to be drawn to dysfunctional black men and especially in white families that have a problem with black men to begin with?* Then the family acts as though, if she had a preference for white men, they would not have problems, instead of just accepting the fact that she has low self-esteem and would choose poorly no matter what race the package is wrapped in.

I am still nursing the same glass of white wine I poured an hour earlier. Everyone has eaten, and the music is playing a bit louder than before. Music is great for staving off awkwardness. Danny is towering over everyone, at six feet, two inches tall, he is noticed by everyone. My cousin passes me on her way to the kitchen, "Cousin he's a fine one...that's a good look cuz." She smiles and nudges my shoulder. I feel proud that she sees me as better. I don't know if her comment is related to his whiteness or our togetherness as a couple, but I like it nonetheless. I'm the cool cousin who surprises everyone with bringing a white guy home. Not just dating him casually, without having to claim him as I did in the past, but Danny I make visible.

I find it strange that no one is outwardly shocked by Danny's redneck tendencies, by his Podunk vernacular and his constant beer guzzling. These are the things I am most afraid of. I am afraid that my family will be ashamed of my choice like they were with my ex. I am afraid that his lack of education will allow space for ignorant ideas and thoughts that would be best left unsaid, to fall out of his mouth like an avalanche of unintended disrespect. Like they do when it is just him and I. But I don't feel disrespected, his words do not have that kind of power over me. I correct his ignorance and we move on, but not everyone is so forgiving.

The more drinks Danny has, the louder he gets, like the engine of a muscle car revving aggressively with each tap on the gas. The beer being the tap and Danny being the engine. He makes his way across the crowded kitchen to my mother. I can feel he has something to say that may or may not be worth voicing. I do not like feeling the need to guard this man's words, but I take on this role and follow his conversations, like a mother follows behind a toddler learning how to walk. The toddler is not ready to teeter about on his own and neither is Danny. His obliviousness to his white male privilege is too raw and untamed.

"Her ex is a damn fool!" Danny blurts out to my mother. I hear these words through the chaos of the gathering only because I'm honing in on them.

My mother is unsure of what Danny means and she responds with a blank look. He repeats himself. Danny does not care to feel out the energy of the room and know when and when not to speak, or what or what not to say. His energy is like a force to behold, maybe narcissism but mostly just brash.

"Her ex is a damn fool...if he thought she couldn't cook. She's a great cook, the best cook I know, except for my mama!" Danny shouts over the music. I glance over, trying to appear easier than I feel. No anxiety, even though it's been nearly two hours since my last puff. When I'm distracted, I don't need pot or Xanax. This is how I know my anxiety is all in my head, but it is harder to control my thoughts than it is to pop a pill or inhale some smoke.

My mom nods slowly in mock agreement. She is visibly taken aback but Danny does not notice. I can see that she doesn't know how she feels about a white man talking down on a black man so casually. She is not completely race-driven, but I can see that she feels he is disrespectful, that he hasn't earned the right to discuss my children's father and as a white man, he is simply out of line.

For Danny, he is just a new boyfriend standing up retroactively for his new girlfriend. I am also conflicted like my mother, but my conflict lies within my children's father being attacked, because I love them and he is a part of them, which makes belittling him with an outsider, (Danny being the outsider), on any level feels gross and like I'm betraying my daughters. I don't fuel this fire. Danny continues to make his rounds, indifferent about the words he places so carelessly around the room. Like a bull in a china shop, Danny is less than graceful.

When it is time for Danny to leave, Tim is not ready to go. I look into the room where they're playing video games and Tim blends in. The boys bond over strategies and techniques. As my cousin arrived earlier, she nudged her four boys and said, "Y'all know how to act around white folks." She was casual, not joking and moved on as if there was a specific and separate way to act around white people as opposed to anyone else. I ponder heavily, *what could the difference be?* I stop in mid thought, as her three little black boys walk in a single file line into the guest room and think, *this...this right here is how inferiority complexes are nurtured in the home.* I am hurt and annoyed. Hurt that this is a thing and annoyed that I am face-to-face with it. To her, *do white people deserve more respect than we would give to the people who look just like us?* I ponder why so many black people continue to privately acknowledge and perpetuate all the racial stereotypes that ultimately piss them off when directed squarely at them by white people. Generationally, these mistruths are shoved into family conversations where small children are developing and learning, learning that they are the "other" and less than. The adults feel comfortable participating in this massacre of self-esteem, feeling they are preparing them for a world that does not love them, even though love is an inside job that all humans must learn to internalize. *How are her words helpful?*

I'm quickly reminded of the burden of being the forgotten class. The seventy-five perfect of African-Americans who do not live in poverty, who run their own businesses, who are educated, who speak great English, whose children are not delinquents and so forth and so on. We are forgotten in mass media representations and our impoverished counter-part is celebrated. And since people love the simplicity of a single story that fits nicely in a cube as it relates to any group of people, African-Americans in the forgotten class often find themselves trying to make up for *all* the representations of crackheads on the news, drug dealers in top rated television shows, armed robbers, prisoners, child abandoners, prostitutes, the uneducated teen mom and so forth and so on. I know I stack because of this too. Being greater than such small ideas of blackness comes so easy for me. So much so that I feel I would be doing me and the white spaces I encounter a disservice by not using myself as a tool to educate. I would be lying if I said that when I baffle white people, I don't get a kick out of it.

I baffle Danny's family, and this is understandable, it's not right, but it's understandable. Many of his family members that live in the boondocks have little to no interaction with people of color. Their interaction is mass media representations. There are roughly 220 million whites in this country as opposed to roughly 34 million blacks. It seems America as a whole is a white space too.

My family's Thanksgiving is the complete opposite of Danny's Thanksgiving. My home is warm, inviting and loving. Danny notices this difference.

"I had a better time with your family than I did with my own. They ain't nothin like the black people you hear about all the time. Not that it makes a difference that their black, but you know black people...nevermind...I had too much to drink. I can't pull my thoughts together...I might say something wrong." Danny stops and leans against the counter. I display a gentle, exhausted smile. My ability to transcend the limitations of race is a gift and a curse, people sometimes talk to me as if I weren't black. It's like spying in plain sight. The fact that race does not burden my soul with anger allows people to unburden their souls with less caution.

Danny grabs me and with the grace of a caveman, presses his lips against mine, then shoves his beer drenched tongue into my mouth. I am not completely turned off. I remember that we still have not had sex. I am not in a rush because Danny will be the first white man I'll actually have intercourse with. I know I'm going to do it, but I haven't decided when. I am not drawn to him irresistibly because I know he is not *the one*. But intellectually I am curious. I am curious to see if race will make a difference. I am curious about his penis size and the rhythm of his stroke. I am curious to see if he will be in awe of my naked brown body. I am curious about his smell, his moan and the way his body will tighten and release when he reaches his climax. I am just curious.

Danny loosens his squeeze and rests both his hands on the small of my back. Our noses are only a half-inch apart. His eyes gaze romantically into mine. I feel rehearsed. I know how to show interest, I know how to look longingly into a lover's eyes. What I don't understand is how Danny is feeling in this moment. *Is this a deep connection for him? Or is he just resting in the comfort of our space?* I do know that it is peaceful and kind. It is a moment void of all judgment and stacking. That part is real. The authentic experience of human sameness is present. The sameness is what I am falling in love with, not Danny.

Gail's potato salad is not a hit. Turns out Danny may be the only one who thinks it's the best in the entire world.

My brother later tells me that Danny corrected his pronunciation of the word *animal.* My brother said that at the time he paid no mind to Danny repeating the word and annunciating it in slowly. The next day, I mention to him that as poorly pronounced as Danny's redneck English is, he still attempts to correct me and consequently my daughters, who's English is more accurate than all of the adults put together. Then my brother is pissed. I giggle.

"Who the hell does he think he is? Trying to correct my English, has he heard himself talk? He just made an assumption that all black people don't speak good English and we need his help. I wish I would have known at the time, that's what he was doing..." My brother grunts out this rant on the other end of the phone, reminding me of Theo from The Cosby Show. He is so mild-mannered that even his outrage doesn't seem angry, coming off, in most instances, as astonishment or disbelief. Danny definitely stirred in him, disbelief.

JAMEELAH RAOOF

CHAPTER SEVENTEEN

Sex

I want to have sex with Danny before my birthday, which is only a few weeks before Christmas. He confessed to me that he stopped calling right before his accident because he thought we would never have sex. Danny said he really wanted to see what it would be like with a black girl and I didn't seem easy enough.

It's a day or two before my birthday and Danny brings Tim over so they can hang my Christmas lights. I only began to celebrate Christmas once my daughters were born. I married into a very Christian family. After divorce, I wanted to make sure my daughters didn't feel left out around the holidays. Which is how a little Muslim girl who fasted for Ramadan as a kid, prayed five times a day, and who has never had pork in her life, fell into a yearly tradition of hanging lights, erecting decorative trees, and buying too many gifts for her daughters.

Danny's estranged wife, Danielle, is the brunt of many jokes. Danny tells these off-colored jokes in front of Tim and Tim says nothing. I have never known a kid to be so visibly vacant and no one around him sees it as an issue. Tim plays video games, goes to school and asks, "What are we eating?" This is the depth of him. Maybe this is normal teenage behavior. Tim is thirteen and does not talk about girls, or anything else for that matter. He is a replica of his father. Tall, muscular, ocean blue eyes and bright flaxen hair. Danny says that by Tim's age he was really into girls. I offered a cautious, "Maybe he doesn't like girls?" Danny's response is, "He ain't gone be no fairy...he better not be no fairy." I chuckle, only because I hadn't actually heard the word *fairy* used to describe homosexuality in years and it not be meant as a joke.

Danny brings everything he own that's related to hanging Christmas lights. He buys new tools, some extra boxes of lights, outdoor extension cords and a sturdy, metal ladder.

"How do you want them?" Danny and Tim stand outside in front of my home. It's cold but they don't seem to notice. The sun is beaming right into Danny's eyes, he drops the shades that rest on the crown of his head, onto the bridge of his nose. Danny's sunglasses are white brimmed with multicolored, mirrored lenses. I despise them. They remind me of poor white guys from my hometown, who are trying hard to look cool. He's just missing the Ed Hardy t-shirt, and something tells me that he probably has one. Danny is not financially poor. He makes more than $90,000 a year working for the railroad, he owns his own home, has two vehicles, and foots the bill for everything, everywhere we go. His exact words to me at the movies one day were, "You don't ever take out your wallet, not with me you don't." I accepted and smiled. Danny is frugal, but not with me. *He can afford better sunglasses*, I think.

"Just hang the icicle lights around the rain gutters and the others you can just wrap around the trunk of the tree." I point at the over-sized crepe myrtle in my front yard. It towers over my single-story, average, brick suburban home. In the Spring, it blooms in a lively shade of pink, that channels the perfection of *Desperate Housewive's*, Wisteria Lane. I am not too creative with outdoor Christmas lights. The instructions I give Danny are pretty much what I see on average homes everywhere I go. Icicle lights at the edge of the roof and a wrapped tree trunk. I don't care enough to add grazing reindeer or blow-up snowmen like my neighbors down the block.

"Me and Danielle used to do it up big, I mean we had the best decorated house on the block. People would stop on the street and tell us how great our house looked…" Danny goes on boasting about his light hanging abilities. I could see that he misses some aspects of his relationship with Tim's mother, but he has a black and white perspective. If he says something nice about their time together, once he notices, he immediately negates it with something not so flattering about her. He can't fathom a world where neither of them are perfect and no one is to blame for the fact that they just don't work. Its so American to feel obliged to pick a side.

Danny orders Tim around, pointing at tools and lights and extension cords for him to retrieve. My daughters are visiting family and I want to surprise them with lights once they return. Danny is also on a visitation schedule with Tim. He plans to drop Tim off at Danielle's so that once the lights are done, he and I can go to a comedy show.

Danny is impressed by his decor. He leaves all the new tools with me and the unused lights. His generosity is attractive. I like being treated like a princess. There is not a request I make that Danny doesn't hop-to to make happen.

I must admit, I am snooty about shoes. I like when men wear clean shoes. No particular name brand or style, but they need to be clean. To me, if the shoes are clean, everything else falls into place. Danny's shoes are always dirty. He is blue collar and only cleans up when he takes me out. Blue jeans, t-shirts and scruffy work boots. Before he returns, I take a trip to the mall and buy Danny some sleek, brown leather boots, black jeans and a short sleeve button-down. I actively ignore the little voice in my head that's screaming, *like him the way he is* and *don't try to change him.* I don't want to change him; just upgrade him a bit. *He is too attractive to be so rough around the edges.* I think rugged is attractive, but it has its time and place. I want his look to match mine; classy and polished. I feel, with a few minor tweaks Danny can pull off both.

Danny walks through the door with a cotton button-down shirt that's a bit dated, worn blue jeans and dingy white sneakers. My face gets hot. We are running late, so there's not time for me to *casually* show him his new clothes and then *casually* suggest that he wears them tonight. I feel stuck, but I dash out the door and I hop in the car anyway.

Danny doesn't mind if I smoke in his car. The last guy I dated was so uptight that I felt I couldn't be myself around him. But Danny is so comfortable in his own skin that it's contagious. I don't have one single care when I'm with him. I don't watch the way I eat with him, I don't hide my true feelings on any topic and I definitely don't pretend to not be a pothead as I had with the last guy. We are easy. I like easy. As we jump into his little Saturn, the SUV he hadn't wanted me to ride in because it wasn't pretty, I think, *maybe this could be right...after all. I have never been myself with any guy I've ever dated...this is so easy, it just might be right.*

I break my bathroom only rule and bring my pipe and a little pot with me. I have a favorite pipe that's made out of blown glass, uses filters, and cleans with ease. It is a trite Rastafarian red, green, and yellow, but it just happened to be the cheapest style available when I was in the market for one.

I am nervous about going to this comedy show. As much as I don't like to admit it, my easiness with Danny is easier when we're alone. It's the stares. I never thought the stares would get to me so much. It's the blank look on people's faces that make me want to scream. *GET A LIFE!* I can't comprehend why an interracial couple would still get so much attention this day in age.

I puff away my anxiety and listen passively to Danny's country music. I replay in my head, the worst-case scenario at the comedy show until my deep inhales push the useless thoughts to the recesses of my mind, just far enough back to experience some semblance of normalcy.

Once we get to the club the crowd is sparse. This relaxes me. My obsession with being gawked at is all in my head.

"We have VIP tickets babe...they were the same price online as the regular seats..." Danny is proud of his discount. He smiles like he got one over on the club.

"What exactly does VIP mean?" I ask as we stand in the lobby, near the bar waiting to be seated. I scan the room feeling a strange type of discomfort that has never consumed me before. I care deeply about what people think. If Danny were black and dressed the way he's dressed, I'd be slumming. But I think I give him a pass because of his whiteness. I don't know if his style of dress is okay in his world. In an effort to not offend, I just leave it alone and do my best to be less shallow.

This club is not at all a white space. It's quite diverse, but the discomfort is soaring like a kite that I can't get a handle on because I let it go too far for too long. Now the force of the wind is behind it and there is almost no turning back. I start my deep breathing exercises below my breath. *Belly breaths...deep belly breaths*, I think. The music masks my ocean-like exhalations. My underarms are sweating, my heart is racing and stomach churning. I hate feeling like this. I want to scream and run and run and scream, in that order, *but that wouldn't be appropriate.*

I reach down into my bag, feeling for the little pink pill case I mostly keep filled with Xanax. The more my hand swims around the bottom of my bag the more my panic constricts me. I think, *f*ck...I didn't bring any.* I want to cry. I really want to sob uncontrollably. None of this is apparent to Danny or anyone else for that matter. My anxiety is a private affair. I suffer alone and fix it alone. Just when I am ready to give in and ask Danny to leave, the tip of my pointer finger scrapes a piece of hard plastic and I know it's my pills.

I wrap my hands around the little case as if I were drowning in the middle of the ocean and the case is a life preserver. My terror shift towards elation. Just knowing I have them feels so much better. My brain sends a signal of calm throughout my body because it knows the rescue boat is on its way. Soon I'll be out of the treacherous ocean, dry and back on solid ground. I pop two pills and gulp them down with the glass of cheap chardonnay Danny orders for me. I inhale. Danny answered my question about the VIP spots as soon as I asked, but he was drowned out by my mini panic attack, that I just nodded. I don't really want to know. Its best I don't know what to expect.

The bouncer ushers us in, like we're literally VIP. I am such a behind-the-scenes kind of girl that all I can do is contemplate the end of our walk to our table, which happens to be right in front of the stage. And then I contemplate the end of the night, when we can return to the safe space of just him and I.

We are under spotlights. I am so mad that Danny thought it would be fun to sit right in front of the stage. Now everyone sees me. In theory, interracial dating is fine but now I feel so judged. I'd never known how shallow and vulnerable I am in this area and I don't like it. I dated the Mexican guy, but nobody judges a black woman that dates a Mexican. For all they know, I could be Dominican or Honduran. When we were in Puerto Rico together people spoke Spanish to me just like they did to him. But it is clear that me and Danny are from very opposite sides of the track. I feel like I'm in the movie *Something New* when Sanaa Lathan's character meets her white, rugged blind date at the coffee shop and all she wants to do is disappear.

The gawking begins, and Danny enjoys it. As a bonafide extrovert, he is used to being in the spotlight and has no shame in craving attention. He has a talent for saying the most inappropriate things and never noticing the reactions of others. I am severely self-conscious to say the least.

"You look so f*cking sexy baby..." Danny says, leaning across the table to kiss me on the cheek. His peck is like a flag erected on new territory, he has proudly conquered. I am mortified, but my Xanax is working so I just smile and glue my eyes to the laminated menu of deep-fried *everything* in front of me.

I am beautiful tonight. I am wearing a form fitting red dress that stops just above my knees, black heels and my hair in a huge afro puff at the very crown of my head. My makeup is flawless and so is my mani-pedi. I want to go to the restroom just so I can look at myself once more and possibly take a selfie for social media, but I am too afraid to move. Too afraid to trigger my anxiety and have it scream at a volume too loud for correction. I stay put.

"You want anything to eat?" Danny asks right as he downs his third drink of the night. That is, if he started since we've been together. Danny doesn't get sloppy when he drinks, amplified but not sloppy.

"I'm good...but I'll have another glass of wine though..."

"Hey! Hey!" Danny shouts, waving over the waitress who seems less than enthusiastic about being called to our table like a puppy.

"My girl wants another chardonnay and bring me another beer..." Danny slaps his hand against the table like an old cowboy, flashing his Pudunk smile at me. This night, I forget for a moment that Danny and I are officially boyfriend and girlfriend.

The second glass of wine does the trick. I am in the zone, spaced out enough to get through the night. The first comedian comes to stage and I'm ready to let go and giggle my apprehension away.

The comedian is a youngish Hispanic guy who immediately lays eyes on Danny and me.

"I had a great opener for this show but first...what do we have here?" He posts himself directly in front of our table.

"Are ya'll together?" The comedian pretends as if his query is innocent and not leading towards a joke at our expense.

Danny answers swiftly. "Yep!" He flashes that smile.

Not only can I feel the entire audiences' eyeballs on every inch of my skin, but I also know I have nowhere to hide. Crawling under the table would just make me look as crazy as I already feel. This is happening and there is nothing I can do about it. Danny is only five years my senior, but his blue-collar lifestyle adds five additional years to his looks.

"Is there a big age gap between you two?" The comedian chuckles because we are simply a tool to break the ice and for him, this is going quite well.

"None of your business!" Danny shouts back. The audience reacts, and Danny is sucking it all up, grinning from ear-to-ear. My smile is plastered on. I am outside of my body.

"All right Jungle Fever, I'm gonna leave y'all alone!" The audience erupts in laughter as if the phrase, Jungle Fever had just been invented by this comedian, at this very moment. I feel naked...so naked.

"I mean, I love black women, I get it man!" The comedian blurts out. *Now I'm an object belonging to a group of like objects and not a real person,* I think. And these objects, black women, are apparently interchangeable.

"I mean she is fucking beautiful and she's like, a real black woman, with real black woman hair...she don't get her hair in a bag from Big T Bazaar!" He rolls his neck the stereotypical way a token black woman added for comedic relief in all white movies would. The audience erupts in laughter once again. "Dude, made a serious come up! I'm just saying!" The comedian adds.

I relinquish my plastered-on smile. It's time for him to move on, my straight face suggests. For the next few seconds, I replay the entirety of his comments in my head, lamenting on how wrong it is for him to act like real black women don't wear fake hair, how wrong it is for him to act like Danny isn't good enough for me and how wrong it is to minimize me to a fetish in front of a couple hundred people. The comedian treats his confession of loving black women like some secret declaration that most men are too afraid to admit. I feel dirty and I'm ready to go. But I stay. Danny doesn't offend easy, so we definitely aren't leaving on his account.

After the comedian moves on Danny leans in and whispers, "Are you okay?"

"Yep," I answer without hesitation. I want, even more than to disappear, to go back in time and stop this night from happening.

The remaining acts barely look our way. I don't know if it's all in my head or if Danny and I are a spectacle. *You're so fucking insecure*, I think. Once the show is over and we make our way towards the exit, I drop some of the angst from the comedian's shenanigans. The lights come on and I feel on display once again. *I can't believe I got through that.*

We walk quietly to the car. Danny's energy is heightened. He is full of his beer and also a bit of aggravation.

"Did you like the show?" Danny asks while opening the passenger door for me.

"I did, the last guy was really funny." My response lingers. He doesn't really wait to hear my answer before he's already around the car, jumping into the driver's side. His mood is off. I can feel it.

"Fuckin wetback!" He turns the ignition, then shoots a shameful gaze at me, that morphs into a sort of defiant pride almost instantly. Danny is not sure if it is okay to use a racial slur around me if the receiving race is not black. He's trying to see if we can connect and unify against Hispanics since this takes the focus off black-centered racism. I say nothing and just look forward. I know exactly who he is referring to. But unlike Danny, I prefer to be bothered by the comedian's comments and not his ethnicity or race. This is a fundamental difference between myself and Danny. He believes race matters as a factor in character. I just think some people are assholes and some are not.

"I just want to drive fast right now. That's what I'm like when somebody pisses me off and I don't get a chance to get them back. I just want to fuck something up right now...he didn't really bother me, but I didn't like him talking about you like that." Danny shoots a glare at me again, this time he bypasses the shame, deciding that tonight, I get to see this side of him. I'm sure he means that he didn't like the comedian ignoring any depth in me and Danny's relationship, just to objectify my blackness without acknowledging that Danny and I could be more than fuckbuddies. I get it. Danny doesn't like when he's not taken seriously.

Any other ethnicity of woman with a white man would not raise so many gazes. I've read articles that say that American culture as a whole sees black women as being at the bottom of the dating hierarchy, but this is not how I feel. I don't look half-white, I don't wear weaves and I'm not trying to *be white* through my mannerisms. The onlookers are confused about why he is with me when in all honesty, I feel I could have anyone, no matter their race. I feel, I'm doing him a favor stepping over the color line, I am both desirable and desired. But just because I know this, does not mean the average Joe or Jane does too.

No, the average Joe or Jane believes the mass media portrayals, which ignore my sexy, disregards my intellect, believes my hair is not nice because it's not straight and that the only thing I am good for is being the sidekick to the white girl who, by default, is desired by everyone. As I just sit there, on the sidelines, watching and wishing I were her. They live in a world where all white men want blonde, thin and big boobs, and if they step outside of their race, it should only be for an Asian woman or a sexy Latina or a black woman that looks white. This is not the same reaction that is had when a black man is dating a non-black woman. It is assumed that many black men do not want black women, so when he gets a chance, why wouldn't he date outside of his race? What a lucky dog!

Of course, I don't ascribe to any of this, but I'd be remiss if I pretend I am not familiar with this narrative. I am unfortunately familiar with the expectations of the ignorant and the suppositions of the herd. I don't have to buy into this fallacy to know that it indeed exists.

The truth of the matter is that, human beings are highly driven by mass media representations. A beautiful blonde woman, is not more interesting than a beautiful brown woman with a coily fro. However, the blonde has been shown to be the ultimate beauty in magazines, on television, in movies, in advertising, in music videos and in a surfeit of other avenues through which we consume images and ideas from the world around us.

The problem comes when we are bombarded with only one message, one ideology and cultural hegemony occurs. Suddenly, there is only one way a woman can be beautiful and all women who do not fit this mold should either be trying to fit into this overcrowded cube, be flat out rejecting this ideal and any women that resemble it or be salivating over this ideal with envy and jealousy. I am doing none of the above. I know that the blondes' beauty does not negate nor determine my own beauty. In my world, our beauty can harmoniously coexist.

I have officially been Danny's 'girl' for two weeks. He is happy with me and proud everywhere we go. The stares don't bother him the way they do me. Nothing subtle bothers him. He says that he gets furious when he thinks about somebody not treating me right. *He's such a caveman.* I'm not even begging to be protected, but this is his nature. I have never experienced a man so basic in his role as provider and protector. Danny does not string magnificent thoughts together that blow my mind or suggest new must-reads off the New York Times best-seller list, but he is still unbelievably sexy.

Understanding that I am now in a relationship, I move closer to the idea of having sex. This has by far been the longest amount of time I've gone without sleeping with a guy I've been on so many dates with.

A few days before the new year, we catch a late movie and an even later dinner. I feel anticipation this day. Almost like I am plotting the breaking of my virginity. I fall in and out of not feeling as though I know him enough and feeling as though I know everything I need to. It is our contrast that makes me consider he is not worthy enough to have my body; and equally, our contrast is what intrigues me.

We return to my place and silence hobbles around like a third wheel in our space. I put on a movie and ask Danny if he wants the beer he left in my fridge a while ago. He accepts. I head to my bathroom to puff. Marijuana has always been an aphrodisiac for me. I sit on the sofa next to Danny. He does not take his eyes off me the entire time. *He wants it, he wants me.* He leans in for a kiss. By the look in his eyes, I knew it would be a long, deep kiss. I was right. Danny kisses aggressively, always. I don't want to consider my blackness as a factor in his relentless pursuit, since the black men I've dated in the past have wanted the exact same thing; to take me out and f*ck me later. *Why would Danny be any different?* For me, it's about exploration and not exploitation, regardless of Danny's intentions.

Danny's hands and arms quickly envelop my body. He kisses my neck, squeezes my thighs and slowly drags his hand beneath my shirt. His calloused fingers caress both me and nipples into submission. I am in this moment. I am present and this lust is evolving into amazement. I lift up from the couch. The small loveseat can no longer contain the magnitude of heat cultivated between us. I lead him to my bedroom. The short stroll is quiet and measured.

I sit easy on my bed, allowing Danny to pick up where I left off. The contrast of our skin beside each other feels taboo. It's silly, but that's how it feels. Unholy, unhinged, undeniable. We lock eyes. We capture the thrill in each other's gaze. He is fascinated by me. I love to fascinate him. My legs are in happy baby pose. Yoga pays off. He lifts my dress up and my panties come down. We thrust tremendously, loudly, aggressively. I am present. I don't miss this. I hold nothing back. The contrast, its juxtaposition engulfs me. The blue moonlight dances through the blinds. In the darkness we catch short glimpses of each other's bodies. My eyes adjust and I can see him clearly. My legs tremble. I relax them on his shoulders, throwing my ankles around his neck. He continues to thrust. I love this. My whole body shivers with pleasure. I am maxed out. Spent. I grab onto his biceps. The outline of a large vein is pronounced. I examine his body in short snapshots. Danny Ray is sexy. He continues to thrust. *God can he f*ck.*

"Oh shit...got damn your pussy's good girl..." He grunts. Breathing heavy. He wants to consume me. He's about to climax. I won't peak this time and I don't need to. I caress my breasts for him, Danny is on the brink of explosion.

"Ohhhh shit! ...got damn!" His face scrunches. "You're so fuckin hot..." he whispers in exhaustion. I am told by Danny that I am *hot* more times than I can count. His body collapses on top of mine. I let him lay inside of me until he's done. Done being rescued. I lay his head on my breasts. I stroke his golden hair, *it's too soft.* I watch his sweaty back rise and fall in contentment and relief. We lay in silence. Intertwined. Unchallenged and undefined. The contrast is beauty.

I miss the rhythm. Danny can say all the right things, beautiful words, but all with no rhythm. A flow that I've only heard and felt through the lips of black men. When Danny says, *I want you,* it is nothing like the *I want you,* my first boyfriend uttered the day I gifted him my virginity and nothing like the *I want you,* another black boyfriend of mine whispered in my ear when I was angry and he grabbed my upper arm, the chunky part, and spoke it from the core of his being. I felt his words. Black men make seductive music with their words, whether the words are true or not, they feel wealthy. Every non-black guy that I have dated in the past possessed a genuine appropriation of this charismatic talent. In this moment, I lay here wishing Danny had this rhythm.

JAMEELAH RAOOF

CHAPTER EIGHTEEN

My Birthday

It's my birthday and I am turning thirty-five years old. Danny asks me what I want to do and what sort of gift I want.

"I want to buy you something special but not too expensive. I don't make the kind of money I used to, since the accident." Danny says.

We are sitting on my back porch, Danny is on his third beer and I'm grading some papers.

"Really want us to go to Painting with a Twist." I add.

I wait for Danny's reaction. This is outside of his comfort zone. I remind him that he can drink while he paints.

"I went a long time ago with my ex, I don't remember too much about it." Danny adds.

I get excited. He has rarely had to compromise his wants for the wants of a woman. Danny tries with me. He is deeply vested in getting it right with me. I am like a unicorn to him. I defy all the stereotypes about black and about women he has been taught to hold dear and I exceed in character everyone he has known in his life. He thinks my intellect is sexy and to him, it's even more sexy because it's a black woman's intellect. I am like a buried treasure he had the luck to stumble upon. Buried under his poor, generational belief systems and socio-cultural isolation. But I have been frolicking in plain sight the whole time. Only invisible by social design, but seen thoroughly by me.

I choose the paint and wine venue near downtown Dallas. I figure Danny's big personality would be buffered by the bustle of the city streets and the busy minds that occupy them. People in the city think differently, they talk with agendas and have thin boundaries. Everyone is a fast friend, if only for that night. This attitude combined with drinking buffers loneliness too. I'm annoyed with myself because I am not as comfortable with Danny in public as I would like. I have to get high to be relaxed.

Danny arrives on my birthday with a potted flower in hand. Tulips, red tulips. They are beautiful and fresh. I am eager to post a picture of them on my Instagram page.

Danny is not holding any other gifts, but I am not bothered. I am not consumed with my birthday and I am equally not consumed with men buying me gifts. Danny has that Podunk smile plastered across his face.

"Look inside the flowers!" He can't contain himself.

I look, only smiling to mirror his smile.

I look deeper and right beneath the bright red tulips at the base of the shoots lie a sparkly diamond, white and yellow gold watch. The face is mother of pearl. It is dainty and girly. I love it at first sight. Danny watches my face as I find and retrieve my intended gift. My reaction is my *thank you*. He savors my wide eyes and gentle smile. He quietly waits for me to wrap the lovely trinket around my wrist. I thank him by being an excellent receiver, something I've had to practice over the years. Danny exhales.

"I thought you was gonna be disappointed with just the flowers...but I should have known, you're not like that." He chuckles.

I rise to my tip toes and kiss him on his cheek. I smell beer near his mouth.

I wear a short little leopard print dress, black tights, and black boots. Danny has already consumed a few beers before picking me up. Exactly how many...I'm not sure.

I don't bring any wine. I take a few puffs off my pipe before we leave.

"I sure hope you don't have no high hopes for my painting abilities!" Danny is shouting. When he drinks, he is louder than usual. When I'm high, his volume is tolerable.

"It doesn't matter, it's just about the experience...spending time together and enjoying a new crowd." I add.

"...cause I can't paint worth a shit!" Danny shouts.

He doesn't hear anything I say. That's the thing about having the volume on your own stereo up too loud, it's almost impossible to hear anyone else's music.

Danny is the opposite of a sad, divorced dad. He is not divorced yet, but his ex lives with her fiancé. I feel like one in a series of rebounds for Danny. His previous relationship, after his wife, was drama-filled. In that "immediately after" relationship, people tend to repeat the same mistakes, especially if it's too close behind. Too close to see real growth and to have forgiven. With me, it's different, because Danny is different and I am different. His fall not only slowed him down, but it slowed me down too. I felt compelled to stick around, but it isn't hard. Danny is such uncharted territory that every moment is journey into the unknown. The unknown is what is so intriguing, not particularly Danny. Danny's normal happens to be my abnormal. In all regards, he is quite simple.

We arrive at the paint and wine venue. I prepaid for the spots. This adventure on my birthday is my treat. The venue is quiet, only two other couples are present, a black couple who appear very much in love and a couple of thirty something, white women, seemingly ecstatic about drinking in public as opposed to on their couches. The women study Danny and I closely. White women our age always study Danny and me with an unwavering astonishment. I giggle. I can never figure out exactly what they are thinking. They seem to harbor some level of shock, but I am not sure if its shock that I'm with him or shock that he is with me. We find our seats and Danny is talking loudly with the hostess, cracking jokes and asking where the closest store to buy beer is.

I put on my apron and sit. I admire my new watch. This unfolding moment excites me in a new spot of my being. I am beaming through some uncharted territory within myself. So much so that I can't define it for myself. It is everything and then some, but not the *everything* that I know, another *everything* that I'm just getting to know.

Danny leaves to go to the convenience store across the street to buy some wine. He comes back with a six pack of beer, one bottle of red and one bottle of white. The venue is a little more crowded when he returns.

"I didn't know which one you wanted more, I said fuck it, it's her birthday. I'm getting both." Danny settles in.

A beautiful, curvaceous black woman who is sitting alone, chuckles at Danny.

"See what I'm dealing with..." I tell her in that "gotta love him" kind of way, only because she seems to accept our presence without judgement. She seems comfortable in her skin. So, I become comfortable with her.

I pour myself some wine while Danny is across the room talking animatedly with another couple. He is a people person. I, on the other hand, tend to tolerate people as opposed to celebrating them.

The hostess goes around the room asking questions. She can barely get her spiel out before Danny interrupts with jokes. She now seems to be slightly annoyed by him.

"Are you two on a date?" The hostess asks. Everyone in the room quiets down and turn to look at us.

"Nope, we're comedians," Danny says, he chuckles. He thinks he's just making a joke, but the crowd seemed eager to believe that we were anything but a couple.

She says, "cool..." Then moves on.

The evening goes forward. Periodically we banter with the beautiful black woman sitting next to us. Danny's painting is turning out just as he expected, botched, and my painting is uneventful but nonetheless, fits the mold.

Danny has become fast friends with everyone in our immediate vicinity. He tends to annoy people initially then they give in and learn to like something about him quickly. He is his own person and this knowing doesn't change for anyone. They either join him or move out of his way.

We say our goodbyes. Danny opens my door and hops into his Mustang like a rogue cowboy. We notice we're still wearing our aprons and that we forgot our paintings. We laugh from our guts. Danny runs back in, sorts it all out and returns.

"It was fun wasn't it?" I ask.

"It was cool, my painting looks like shit, but I knew it would."

"The people were nice right?" I ask.

"Yep, I think they still think we're comedians though." Danny is amused that his joke took wings.

"The girl next to me could really paint, she was nice too." I add.

"You mean that hot black chick...she had some great tits...if I had the both of you in bed together, I would have some fun." Danny spews this out as impulsive as his driving.

The music stops for me. Sort of like on movies when the DJ stops scratching, and the party goes silent at the exact moment something outrageous occurs.

I am pissed. Not because I am so in love with Danny, but his words are a shot to my self-esteem, the part of me that feels skinny, and underdeveloped and not curvaceous or womanly enough. The world seems so eager to convince women that they are mentally ill, that all their insecurities are born out of nothing and simply a direct reflection of their own choices. But its more than that. I am out with a guy who thinks it's okay to say things like that and he has never had to adjust his mindset in all of his forty-one years. He doesn't even know how painful his words are and he never had to know.

Most often, white privilege is more like white male privilege and white women have been along for the ride, an incidental partner, reaping both the benefits and burdens of being attached to a man who is never forced to see himself.

I think, *I need yoga in the morning to combat this negative feeling.*

"Why do you think it's okay to say something like that to me?" I demand. I can feel our first fight blossoming in its early stage of development. I can't stop it. It's like a boulder at the top of a very steep hill and his response will either tip the boulder down that hill or stop it before it gains momentum. I want him to pay for all the men who ever made me feel small and for all the times I've felt not good enough. I give him my entire life's pain in this area, whether he can bear the burden or not.

"What did I say?" Danny is genuinely shocked by my reaction. He knows what I'm talking about but refuses to give it the same attention I have.

The rest of the ride is silent. I hold back my tears. And these are *my* tears, they have nothing to do with Danny. I feel a pain he wouldn't began to understand.

We arrive at my house and I am not feeling him staying over at the least bit. Danny is bombarded with discomfort. We move around each other awkwardly. Silently. Not sure of whether a disagreement for us means the end or a new beginning.

Danny stands in the middle of my galley kitchen as I wash some dishes that had been waiting for me all day.

"Well I'm going to go ahead and go. You don't seem like you want me to be here so I'm gonna head out." He waits for my feedback.

I don't want him to stay, but I don't want him to leave under these circumstances either. But I'm exhausted with my thoughts and consequently, his presence.

"Okay..." I never look up.

Danny is bothered.

"I don't like this, maybe you and I need to take a break to see if we really want to be with each other. Maybe we're better behind closed doors than we are in public." He stands in my garage on the way to his car. I am leaning on the doorsill trying to feel something deep, and all I feel is complacency. I don't know how to desire a man so deeply that it aches anymore. My marriage ripped that part of my heart out of me.

Danny stares in my direction, discombobulated, and all I can think about is getting up for yoga in the morning.

JAMEELAH RAOOF

CHAPTER NINETEEN

Why is yoga so white?

Yoga is my tool, my second drug of choice. It softens my thinking like pot but keeps me fit too. I breathe deeply during yoga I flow, I balance, and I grow. My studio has a western approach to yoga. It's more about looking beautiful and working out, than it is about connecting, breathing and becoming centered. I don't mind this approach because I make my practice about what I need for me. I've been to many studios with many different approaches and many different socioeconomic environments. The one constant is that yoga is dominated by twenty to forty-something-year-old white women with similar body types. Thin.

They are nice, but they seem angry. Angry because they're seemingly perfect lives don't feel so perfect, angry because they're not married or angry because they can't stop being envious of their friends. I'm not even sure why, but just angry, but quite nice nonetheless. They all sound the same. They all dress the same. They all drive the same types of cars. Teslas, Beemers, Rovers, Benzs, etc. The mommies are too cool for minivans. No, they don't fall into the minivan, mommy jeans crowd. They saved themselves from that fate with Lululemon, yoga and kale.

They are so white, more-white than they understand. Women of color have to dip their toe into white culture to connect with white women. It rarely works the other way around. Since white women generally monopolize yoga, it is not necessary for them to step outside of their bubble, their comfort zone. One of the younger instructors consistently plays rap music that uses the word nigger. Without thought, just unconscious, unchallenged.

Yoga is expensive because of these women. Because they are willing to pay so much money to enjoy the western version of yoga, the western version of yoga is expensive. It's for the well-to-do, the privileged. These women represent that crowd. For an eastern practice, born out of a second world country, the fundamentals being taught are anything but that. Its exclusive and has transformed into something white women feel they are the authority on. It's their world, I just visit.

~

A few days pass and I feel Danny has moved on. I try to feel bad but a part of me feels like it has been coming to this point all along. A part of me is always one foot out the door because we are so different, and our lives are different, and our families are different. Outside of his whiteness, we are just different. I am engaged in playing with my children and cleaning up behind them when the text alert on my phone dings about ten times in a row. After the children become done with me and distracted by something more interesting, I sneak off to my bedroom to unwrap his words. The text notification symbol is like a little gift box, containing desire, expectation, forgiveness and possibly, hope. I am curious and pleased that Danny is still here, still floating in my space and still willing.

Danny: I miss you.

Danny: I was selfish. We became such good friends that I stopped trying to impress. I took your kindness for granted.

Danny: You make me want to be a better person.

Danny: I know there is better than me out there, but I'm willing to show you that I can be better too.

Danny: I don't even remember what I said to upset you. I know I can be an asshole when I drink.

Danny: I haven't done this dating thing in so long that I'm still trying to figure it out.

Danny: That wasn't the only time I didn't treat you right and I want to make up for that.

Danny: I do think you are special enough to fight for, but I don't want you to feel bad when you're with me.

Danny: Any chance you're ready to talk?

Danny: ???

I stare at the screen. Rereading. Analyzing. Comprehending. Organizing. I think, *this is my way out, this is my opportunity to just end this rollercoaster of newness, emotion and discomfort. I don't have to be so black all the time if I'm not in Danny's world. I don't have to give so much attention to something I can choose to disregard. I can put race back on the backburner, hell, I can just take it off the stove all together. I can just be me. Yasminah.* I spend a few more moments in contemplation before I respond.

Me: In what ways do you take me for granted?

I mostly ask this because I don't feel taken for granted or mistreated. Just misjudged for being too damn cool about everything. In that moment, I wonder if there is another level of better treatment I could be receiving from him, but I have no idea. He's good enough and better than many.

Danny: I need to always try. I don't want the kind of relationship where I feel I don't have to try.

To me, not trying is my goal in all relationships. I don't like him trying. I want him to just be. But him just being is not someone I'm willing to date.

Danny: I want a relationship that never loses excitement.

Me: You can be a bully and an asshole when you drink.

I want him to say he'll stop drinking.

Danny: I know, it goes back to me wanting my way all the time and not caring about the repercussions of that.

Danny: I have great will power and when someone is important to me I can do anything.

Danny: And yes, I want that someone to be you.

Danny: I still want to be me, but just more considerate.

Me: Prove it.

I am still waiting for him to say he'll stop drinking, but I have known Danny long enough to know that he does not make promises he does not intend to keep. He does not intend to stop drinking. I think, *well it was wishful thinking.* I want to tell him that he is on borrowed time as drinker but it sort of feels like mucking up the divine order of things. I don't want to threaten or push. And I'm okay with walking away when I've had enough of him.

Danny: You've already changed me so much, I just hope you get to be the one who enjoys it.

Danny is a narcissist. He is a nicer narcissist than my ex, but a narcissist nonetheless. My presence is in his world, he is not in mine. He does not feel his whiteness when he is in my space. He is the same him everywhere he goes. He does not need to consider his whiteness when entering my neighborhood or interacting with my children. His whiteness provokes no insecurity in him in any environment he frequents. This truth coupled with narcissism makes him the quintessential embodiment of white privilege, if such a thing exists. I feel human privilege. I feel privileged to live a life of freedom and choices on a daily basis. I feel privileged to have my life, my children, my health and my career. But in the superficial world of race over everything, I am often forced to participate in tapping into my less than human aspects, like female, black, homeowner, professor, etc. In my hierarchy of personal identification, all of those labels pale in comparison to being human.

I am not done with Danny. I am not done conquering myself and who I am in his presence. I want to know and understand the me that likes that he is white, that feels taboo and edgy because of it.

I don't date white men because I believe they are better than black men. It's like graduating from college, *magna cum laude*. The primary reason is to further your career, but if people prop you up on a pedestal because you have the degree, that's kind of nice. The world is kinder, more patient and more respectful to white men than it is to black men. I gain a companion and subsequently, a mate without boundaries. This is my ugly truth.

CHAPTER TWENTY

She Didn't Say Shit

On Christmas Eve Danny comes over to assemble this elaborate, plastic doll house I purchased for my children. There are over 200 plastic pieces and Danny is delighted to take this on. If I'm being honest, I don't trust him with this expensive dollhouse. I watch him yank the parts out of the box with pure vigor and machismo. He takes his macho nature everywhere he goes. Him, juxtaposed against the soft, pink colored doors, stairs and windows makes me giggle. Danny still does not have feeling in his fingers on the damaged hand. I can see the fingers barely bend the same as they were the night we painted. I am conscious of his limitations with his hand but he doesn't acknowledge it. He lays all the parts in one big pile, then flips the instructions over fast, without reading. He glances at them to see if they are malleable to his style and the way he thinks but the instructions fail miserably. I anxiously watch them get tossed aside.

I walk away and I puff. I try to take a back seat to something a man *should* do since I have been told nearly all my life that I have too much masculine energy. That I am too handy, too resourceful, too intelligent and too wise to attract a man and keep one. I have been told this only by black men who were either related to me or treated me as a friend. I try to figure out why it is so easy to trample on a man's ego (at least the ones that I interacted with), to make him feel small and unimportant. I want to see if Danny is like this, but I don't test the waters, I just step aside. I want to believe that because he is white, he does not see me that way. That he sees my sexy, my femininity, my warmth and my beauty first. I want to believe that he has not been exposed to those stories about black women that have been planted, cultivated and harvested amongst blacks. I hope no one else knows these stories that lend to black women being incapable of femininity, submissiveness and tenderness.

In my mind, these are lies, based on a strict definition of femininity and tenderness that was manufactured and filtered through whiteness. I think, *why does their definition have to apply to everyone else? Why can't I be the backbone and the nurturer, the mechanic and the housewife, the knowledge seeker and the freak in the sheets? And why does my greatness cancel out the greatness of black men? Why am I responsible for him knowing his worth?*

Danny is going on about Ben and his ex. He has no idea the level of depth that is charging through my brain. He has no idea that I am merely an observer of *Yasminah* and her interactions in this world and I am not in the muck like he his. He has no idea that I am not capable of taking my human experience so personal, and finite. He is just here, and I appear to be just here too.

We visit his nuclear family of origin on Christmas day. His mom, aunt, sister, her husband, one cousin, her husband and their children. I bring my children along. I'm not sure of where me and Danny's relationship is headed but I do know that it can go anywhere without the emotional consent of my children. I am ready to enter the lion's den again, but it is nothing like I imagine. It is the same as the time Danny and I visited a friend of his and his wife on their farm. Danny tells me right before we pull into their obnoxiously long driveway, that his friend's wife said, "Danny better not bring no niggers to my house." Of course, Danny brings me anyway. He says, "She ain't gonna say shit! I promise you. They'd rather hate people behind their backs." And Danny was right, she didn't say shit, she didn't frown, hide or complain. So, for Christmas, I figure it would be much of the same. Which might explain why racism has always felt like chasing a ghost to me or like a thick fog that disappears the closer you get to it. You can stand right in the midst of it with only the essence of its vapors surrounding you, but there is nothing tangible to latch on to. It's the nature of something as fleeting and superficial as racism, not having the solidity to be confrontable in a three-dimensional space, rarely is the fog thick enough to know unequivocally that you are standing squarely in the midst of it. That there are no other explanations, interpretations or sensitivities present. I decide that I can't *know*. And if I do, *what does it change?,* I ponder. Me knowing that I am in the midst of fog does not change whether or not I am enveloped by it.

I see Danny's family as only one thing. These are the people Danny had referred to as stone cold racists, who frequently used the "N" word, complained about not wanting to live anywhere near blacks and how black people had it easy being able to collect welfare, food stamps and live in section 8 housing. Of course, these rants are littered with miseducation since blacks only make up twelve percent of the population, it is nearly impossible for them to be the largest recipients of government services. This I learned while researching rural poverty in America. Which boiled down to white poverty in America, and the numbers were staggering. It seems urban poverty is much more appealing in all facets of media.

These people, Danny's family did the same as his friend's wife. They welcomed us, were kind and showed no signs of any of the behavior Danny had shared with me early on.

His family home is a double wide trailer. I think, *what have I gotten myself into? What have I gotten my children into?* The trailer is stationary, more like a fabricated home. I stand in the kitchen waiting to serve myself a piece of turkey, when I overhear Danny's sister complain about how her food stamps were reduced and that she's not getting enough hours at her grocery store job. She is on the phone in the wash room, having what she thinks is a private conversation. I think, *my stacking would be wasted here.*

One of Danny's cousins buys my daughters gifts. They open them with bouts of skepticism and then my youngest takes off her mask of caution completely. She rips into the package, elated that this trip held a surprise for them. Danny watches smiling from across the room. They receive stuffed animals and quietly say thank you. By now I'm over the trailer and the whiteness doesn't feel as thick. We chat at the dinner table, make a few jokes. The frame of commonalities sweep over the space. Only once did Danny's aunt, who's husband is in construction, have to catch her words when she says, "if you can't get Mexican's to do cheap work for you, you're in trouble." Every adult in the vicinity, look away, it gets cold and sobering. I don't feel this is inherently an untruth, especially in Texas, but if I'm being honest, it's her southern twang, her whiteness and the way its said that feels yucky. I remember, *oh yeah, I'm black first to them.* I don't know how I should feel about her, so I choose to feel nothing.

~

On New Year's Eve I share with Danny that I write books.

"You write, like real books you can read?" Danny asks, his eyes concerned.

"What other kind of books are there?" I giggle. We are walking out of a Chili's restaurant near my home. We had planned to go to one of those big New Year's Eve ball's in downtown Dallas, but Danny neglected to buy the tickets early. Dressed to impress, we head to Chili's instead.

"I mean like, you can buy them in the store?" Danny provides clarity.

"Yes, novels..." I wait.

"I don't know how I get a woman like you." Danny shakes his head. He opens the passenger side door for me.

"I don't read...I mean I know how to read, but I don't read books, so I'll probably never read your books. I got a cousin that likes to read, though." Danny adds. He admires my intellect but pays no real attention to it.

We bring in the new year cuddled on the sofa at my place, watching a movie, an

action movie that I can barely keep my eyes
open for.

CHAPTER TWENTY -1

Social Media

I have two personal social media accounts; Instagram and Linkedin. I pride myself on not having a personal Facebook page since I feel like the vast majority of it is porch sitting, pretention and gossip. Facebook feels like going home to visit old friends and family and for me, that's only tolerable if I do it less often.

Danny has a Facebook page that he barely uses, especially since his accident. I use my Instagram vigorously and unapologetically. I display my politics, my authentic likes and dislikes, my new outfits, my new hairdos, etc. I am simple and mediocre on Instagram. It is my soft place to fall since the Facebook crowd hasn't made their way to it. While I am fast and free on Instagram, I am picky about what gets posted. There is a meme floating around that says, "post a picture of us on your social media so I can know it's real." While the Internet used to be viewed as this magical place where you could lie and scheme and pretend to be someone else, over the past five years, it has grown into a solid social setting. Just as solid as the neighborhood bar or the break room at the workplace. It's a casual environment where we can introduce new and exciting life changes, so when it comes to introducing my new and exciting romance I am hesitant. *Will I look like a sell-*

out for dating a white guy? Will I look like one of those self-hating, white aggrandizing, natural hair wearing black chicks? I think.

Social media is not only about who we are, and what we like, but it also gives other's insight into how we would like to be perceived. Since it is a choice, what we post is even more pronounced. I choose to post a picture of Danny and me. First, because I don't want to care about how I am judged for my personal decisions and second, because I like spending time with him and he is a part of my life, so why not?

I post a picture of Danny and I from New Year's Eve. I am wearing all black and so is Danny. I choose a picture that disguises any redneck attributes he might exude. I post and I wait. I wait for my heart to stop racing and for the comments to roll in. Social media is like that. It feels like the whole world is looking, lurking, and waiting for your post. But it is not. They are not. No one really cares about what you post until, on some off chance, they do.

Like after like, I become more relaxed, more comfortable with my choice of Danny, my choice to post him and my choice of picture. Comments roll in, "That's a good look!" someone says. I wonder what she means. I stare at the comment hoping that the meaning behind the comment jumps out at me. *Is she saying that white men are better than black men? I hope not, because I do not feel that way.* I realize that I am sensitive about xenocentrism. I am sensitive about whether I am xenocentric and do not know it. I am, indeed, a product of black perceptions in a sea of whiteness and I do not know how much of my attraction to Danny is real and how much is fabrication. Then I walk away from these thoughts, understanding that I have no desire to always think like the perpetual underdog.

The next day, and the day after, I post him again and again. Each time with a subtitle that reads, "Me and my favorite guy…" along with whatever activity we find ourselves engaged in. In between these posts are pictures of my natural hairstyles and yoga poses. I want the world to see me as adventurous before they consider me lost.

~

When I am in front of an audience, I am not any of the pieces of me that hold me hostage, I am only those pieces that set me free. Beyonce has Sasha Fierce and I have Professor Bashir. Professor Bashir is quiet perfection. She was born to handle the delicate nature of complex subject matters and morph them into simplistic nuggets of truth (or vastly agreed upon opinions). She turns the big into something bite-sized, tolerable, digestible. I am proud that I get to share the same physical body as her. Professor Bashir is impressive, I hover above her when she is in action, with pure admiration and gratitude that I get to masquerade as her. I get to enjoy the fruits of her labor, accept accolades on her behalf and receive the love that she has cultivated. I am everything because of her.

CHAPTER TWENTY-2

Honky-Tonk Bar

Danny is taking me out. He is super excited about seeing one of his favorite bands in concert. The venue is a large dance hall about an hour outside of Dallas. This is a small-town night club where everybody knows everybody. Danny's roommate Lonny and his new girlfriend Jackie are double dating with us. Lonny uses online dating and his baby face to pick up a new woman just about every other month. I have already seen three short-lived relationships come and go.

Danny is annoyed that online dating allows someone like Lonny to pick up a *heap of chicks*. Danny's words, not mine. This is Danny's role in their friendship. He discusses Lonny's constant rotation of bed mates with disgust, as if it is not a lifestyle he ascribed to for many years, before and during marriage.

Danny tells me that he and his ex were swingers. They allowed many different couples into their marriage bed. I never ask about the extent of the sexual activity because it is a territory I choose not to explore neither physically or vicariously. He tries to talk about it often, but I find a way to change the subject. I appreciate his honesty, still.

The night of the concert Danny is dressed in full gear. The cowboy hat, the plaid shirt, the slim-fit jeans, expensive boots and a buckle so large it could double as a weapon.

I see him in his native get up and think, *Danny is fine as fuck.* It is no wonder he has never had to see himself. I realize I am dating the popular guy. The guy who is never told no and who can have who he wants, when he wants. This is especially true for women his age. They throw themselves at him and he allows his masculinity to paint him oblivious. But he is not.

We take a few pictures before we leave. I'm wearing some high-waist, fitted, leave-nothing-to-the-imagination pants, black boots, and a cropped black wrap. My hair is in two-strand twists. Lonny snaps the photos. I post them to Instagram.

The dance hall parking lot is overflowing and huge. We drive across a gravely surface before pulling into one of the unmarked spots. The sound reminds me of driving through trailer parks from home. I feel awkward, so very awkward.

I know I am judged for this relationship. By my family especially. But its them who have no stories, no experiences of being around people who are not like them. People who challenge their long-held norms and beliefs. People whose mere presence stretches them, where the comfort zone does not exist, is not even in the vicinity.

In this Podunk town, nearly an hour outside of Dallas, my comfort zone is not even on the map. But I am here.

"You ready for me to show you some of my moves?" Danny is serious about creating an experience for me that I have never seen before. He wants to introduce me to something new, but that is already happening. This moment of fear and excitement all meshed into one is happening.

I nod. "Oh Lord, I can only imagine." I respond just to respond.

Danny holds my hand, interlocking his fingers between mine, squeezing periodically. I don't squeeze back.

The dancehall is about $25 to get in. I believe it is gouging its patrons for lack of anywhere else to go. I stand back, as always and Danny reaches for his wallet without thought.

The stares began. I feel so out of place. I know that my awareness is super heightened because I'm high, which is also why I am not outwardly phased.

"Have you ever been here before?" Lonny's girl Jackie asks. The men walk together behind us. By default, we should talk. I can tell she is baffled by me. She tries to start a conversation but is not sure of what direction to go. She can see that I am not "hood", nor am I trying to "act white", this is confusing for many including Jackie.

The music playing is gutter. It's rap of some sort. I like to call it pop-rap. The type of music that is not in alignment with the oversized confederate flag stretched generously across the back wall of the dance floor. I see hip-hop as music that evolved from urban, over-crowded pain, sporadic and episodic and country music evolving from rural, lonely pain, deep and long-suffering; both valuing the underserved and overlooked. I think, *working-class people of all races have a lot in common*. I look around at the hundreds of people and none look like me. This is authentically a white space. I feel like a bird of paradise in a room full of lilies. One is no more beautiful than the other, but you would definitely notice the bird of paradise first.

We round the dance floor and settle on a standing table near the floor. The band is setting up their equipment and Danny is talking non-stop as he always does. He tells me that I'm a good listener and I think instead that I'm just good at being quiet. I don't understand half of what he says but he doesn't make a habit of checking in for response or agreement.

The music switches to Taylor Swift. The young people dash to the dance floor. The young men are in blue jeans and plaid shirts, only a few with hats, but all with boots. Danny is bothered by their lack of cowboy attire at an establishment he frequented in his twenties, where the dress code was once strictly enforced. The young ladies are all in floral prints, it looks like a Lucky Brand Jeans ad.

"I don't see how they let them in with no hat and their shirts not tucked in..." Danny shouts towards Lonny over me and Jackie's heads.

Lonny hunches his shoulders. His standards for the outside world are a lot lower than Danny's. Lonny is the kind of man who walks into the room and immediately looks for the sign with the rules of conduct posted. Danny is the type of man who walks in a room and stands with his back turned to said sign and makes his own rules. I believe a little bit of both is good.

Earlier in the evening Danny informs me that Jackie "has money". This seems to be a bonus in Lonny's eyes. Both men often complain about women being gold diggers, especially women who are beyond forty. Jackie volunteers to pay for she and Lonny's drinks and Danny shakes his head in disapproval. Danny is frugal, but when he does take me out, he never expects that I should pay for anything.

The band begins to introduce themselves. Danny shouts and whistles along with the crowd before the band finishes. They receive a warm welcome.

"This band would be more popular if the lead singer was better-looking!" Danny shouts.

I look at the lead singer and think he is more ruggedly handsome than Danny, but his eyes are not blue, and his hair is not blonde, which seems to be the vastly agreed upon standard of beauty in white spaces.

Their music is sort of folksy and mostly country. I like it. Danny wants to take me on the dance floor but song after song he decides that the melody isn't right or there's too many people on the floor or that he needs to finish his drink. His liquid courage hasn't kicked in, but he would never admit this.

I have grown immune to the stares, my liquid courage is working just fine. Danny swoops me up and charges toward the dance floor without saying a word. His dancing is consistently the same move. The couple moves around the perimeter of the dance floor doing two steps and twirl...two steps and a twirl...and on and on.

A few of the onlookers can't stop looking. They want to look away but we do command a lot of attention. I think, *I have rarely experienced the whole, "go back to where you come from vibe".* The only other memory I have of feeling this way was growing up on my street, having to walk by the yards of some very old and openly racist white people. They were half-dead but always had enough energy to snarl and roll their eyes at small black children. Even then, I thought they seemed silly, now I know they were.

I feel that vibe tonight. Before we walk off the dance floor, one of those strange stares walks over and declares, "You have a great ass!" I smile. Danny pulls me away from her. "She's wasted." He adds. I guess if I were from that town and surrounded by those people and of course white, the first thing I might compliment a black girl on is her ass too. After all, black American hip hop not only reeks of pain and "look at me, I'm so flashy I won't be ignored", it also has turned the black female ass into a spectacle separate from the women they are attached to. I wonder if this objectification is birthed out of generations of ancestors being bought and sold based on their physical abilities and not their intellect.

Its another one of those, *not your fault, but definitely your problem* scenarios. I remember once watching this YouTube vlogger that framed her world travel experience as a "black woman who travels". *As if black women don't travel,* I always thought. But she had a huge following, nonetheless, of women who placed their difficulties with traveling squarely on their race and their fear of how they will be received in other countries. The vlogger told a story about sitting in a café in Germany and being asked to duplicate some black American female stereotype a few young German guys had seen on WorldStar. She poked fun at how ignorant people are worldwide reminding her followers to not be too disappointed with insensitive, dumb questions. She also said in that moment, she glanced around the café and noticed no one in the crowded space looked like her, but she found even more isolation in that fact that no one else was from America. The vlogger said she felt even more empty not having a cultural mate than someone who just shares her skin color.

This is the same way I feel with Danny, that more than anything, he is not my cultural mate.

CHAPTER TWENTY-3

What is white American culture?

In my world, American culture *is* white culture, hence the clunky ethnic title of *African-American*. I think, *what if we go around referring to whites as European-American?* It would seem as though the person is a foreigner from Europe, who is now an American citizen. I guess this is why I prefer just American. You can look at me and see that I'm black. Before knowing I'm American, you will know that I am black.

White culture is mainstream culture. Even when music, food and clothing from minorities influence mainstream culture, it is often so watered down that calling it by its influencer would not do it justice. Like referring to pop-rap as Hip Hop. One is a peripheral off-shoot, but in no way a substitute for the original.

White culture is the default. Everything that is anything is always compared to white culture as a means to validate, measure up or illegitimate minority efforts: such as fashion choices, hair styles or vernacular. Preppy clothes are preferred over urban, straight hair is preferred over kinky and "fixin to" is more socially acceptable than "finna" (both poor English). It often seems the more white/mainstream American culture minorities adopt, the more they are seen as a "model minority".

I'm so exhausted with whiteness. I can barely study anything related to my field of study without the backdrop of global whitewashing cloaking every word of the text books, the same way light fills a room. It's there in the interspaces, everywhere you don't look and everywhere you do. It's like I step out of my front door and inhale a deep whiff of whiteness and exhale something akin to a murky grey matter. I'm whitewashed just by my sheer existence. This doesn't make me want to be white, I would assume even whites get tired of experiencing so much whiteness everywhere they go too. My very participation in the western, university setting is a practice of whiteness, no matter how much I rationalize my desire to participate to mean something else.

I once joked about this with Danny in a text message. I told him he forgot to tell me Happy Black History month. He replied by saying he didn't know he was supposed to and sorry for not knowing. I chuckle because of how easy it is to trick a person who has never had to know anything about your culture. Then he replies back, "well, when is white history month?" I reply, "babe, that's all the rest of them."

Even black spaces are white spaces, since they only exist as a counterculture to the white spaces that denied access and rejected black existence. Even whites who don't ascribe to whiteness are deemed as "others". Danny has otherness written all over him. He possessed no white spaces skills or for that matter, he doesn't even acknowledge the backdrop. He knows that looking white is enough to be enough, even if being white garnered no interest in him. His skin was his proverbial plane ticket to ride coach, but he saw no real difference in sitting in first class as long as he was on the plane. He understands his privilege even if he ignores it.

Once Danny recounted a story of visiting the doctor's office and having his first and last name called out only to find that it was the black man on the other side of the room the receptionist was referring to. He chuckled about how interesting it was to have a black man and a white man with the exact same name and that this must have meant his family possibly owned the black man's family during the times of the antebellum south. I quickly chimed in, "only prosperous whites owned slaves, those who could afford it, while many lived in a slave society where blacks were subjugated and stripped of their ancestral identities, many poor and middle class whites barely owned their own homes." *They owned their whiteness*, I think to myself. I don't say this.

My comment is sobering. Danny is confused about who I am. I can see his reluctance recognize depth of intellect I truly bring to the table. It bothers him.

Black skin is sobering. It introduces a reality that many white spaces would rather not address. Its visible and visceral, triggering a blood memory that is so much easier to endure if blackness is ignored or forgotten. And largely it is. White spaces train themselves to reject black skin as the *other* (I don't see race), instead of allowing it to introduce the possibility of a conversation where the experiences might be different, and it just might be because of skin color. And that's okay. The world will not end. Sympathy, fear and/or rejection are not the only choices for white spaces when confronted with black skin. Respect is okay too.

CHAPTER TWENTY-4

Off-Roading?

Life is about the being, not the doing. I am enough without the stacking, without the external approval and without a man. I am perfect, I am happy, I am whole and I am blessed. I hold a deep knowing of the significance of my value.

I am screaming and shouting and belting. The rain is powerful, strong, heavy drops the size of marbles. It is pitch black outside. The two-way road has disappeared into the fierceness of the rain. On this path, there is a series of large ponds with tight, little two-way bridges to cross them. There is no visibility. Danny continues to take the old Bronco off-road to prove that the storm can't smother his fire.

"Don't you dare Danny! Get back on the road! I have children!" I bark these phrases out hysterically over and over again. Danny continues to head off the road and into a grass area down below. There no seatbelts. We are being bumped around the back seat. I bark louder. I don't care how crazy I may seem to them. Danny is not hearing my discomfort, my cries for help. I feel pissed and invisible. I feel ignore and angry. I can barely breathe. Lonny is playing it cooler than he feels. His date is beginning to follow my lead. Danny can't see out of his right eye too well but he is so fuckin determined to be a bad boy that he puts all our lives in jeopardy. The

Bronco titls back and forth, the rain even seems to be angrier. I think, What if we fall into the water? What if we sink? What will my daughter do without a mother to love them? How could I have been so fucking stupid to get into this truck with Danny?

I feel raw, naked and violated like we're involved in an act of sadomasochism and he is ignoring my safe word, my stop word, my panic word. The truck bumps along an unpaved path for the longest two minutes I have ever endured. We arrived at the edge of a wooded area. The threat of falling into water is over. I am silent. Everyone is silent. They are all digesting the terror we had just suffered. Lonny's date exhales slowly, gazing out of her window. I am too pissed to show the relief I'm experiencing on the inside.

Danny takes a short windy road that leads to the main highway. The powerful downpour has passed. Rain storms are quick here, like the wrath of an angry toddler appeased as quickly as their wrath had begun. I can see through the windshield. It's not perfect vision but the night is visible. For the rest of the ride back to Danny's place there was silence and country music. Ironically the song was about a guy back-roading with his favorite girl. I'm guessing Danny didn't see his plans to back-roading turn out this way. The song doesn't give an account of the woman who is the center of the singer's devotion. It doesn't say whether she is enjoying herself in his little one-sided, back-road fantasy. This white space is hick, I come to the conclusion that I do not like hick white spaces. This experience does not bring me prestige, I am not better than anyone by telling this story, and this is not the type of cultural capitol white spaces are supposed to open me up to.

Danny is silent too, which is not common for him. As we cross the threshold and step into his home. He stands still for a bit. He leans on his counter top, grabs a cookie, and begins to chomp on it aggressively, staring straight ahead into clear space.

"I just realized something..." Danny says swallowing the remainder of the cookie. "You don't trust me."

I want to say, *of course I don't, I don't trust any man with my life. It's not personal.* But instead I say, "I do trust you, but I couldn't see anything and you weren't listening to me. You can't do that. You have to acknowledge my cries for help. I told you that I don't take Xanax and smoke pot because I'm a party girl. It provides a thin slice of sanity between me and my anxiety. You can't disrupt that sanity. It's all I have."

He listens but he is hung up on my first sentence. He knows what trusts looks like and me trusting him is not what he witnesses.

JAMEELAH RAOOF

CHAPTER TWENTY-5

Pillow Talk

Me and Danny's pillow talk leads us to mysterious lands, where judgement is not law and answers are neither wrong or right, good or bad, soft or hard. In the wee hours of the morning, before alarms ring, thoughts harden, and cubes solidify. It is freedom.

We discuss tv ads and tv shows that seem to be over-flowing with images of black women coupled with white men, we question if we are playing out a taboo fetish of power and otherness. We express our mutual disinterest in being anybody's social experiment, while knowing full well intertwining our lives is anything but business as usual. I chuckle about a movie preview about a white man loving a black woman, which makes him the shame of his family, and the uncomfortable looks on Lonny and his girlfriend's faces as we all sat in Danny's living room having a double date. Danny doesn't chuckle, but that same uncomfortable look that he had that night settles on his face when in mention it. The longer that movie preview lasts, the more I realized how much being black would always be the pink elephant in the room. I tell him how I love to be better than others and how sometimes I feel so guilty for having the audacity to be black in white spaces. It's not that I don't feel it's okay to be black, I feel it's not okay to be black in some white spaces. I hear a little voice that lingers in my mind, *how dare you bring the awkwardness that is blackness into this happy white space where otherness creates more contrast than this space can quietly maintain.*

Danny doesn't get these thoughts or why anyone would consider their color before occupying a space, even if they weren't welcome. I love his "fuck 'em", cowboy perspective. It feeds the renegade and the queen in me that I am not always sure I have the right to unleash. I unleash all of me with Danny. I am filling every nook and cranny of my space; like water I am pouring generously, thoroughly, and gracefully into my shape, my niche, my gifts, my territory. I am leaving no land untouched, no land unloved. I am whole, and I am full. My cup runneth over and I have surfeits of all of me to give. I am leaving no money on the table, not taking any shorts or losses. Lack of acknowledgement doesn't negate that I'm still here. Danny gets this, and he allows it, knowing that his power is stunted in my space. He gets to witness it but never creates, controls or defines it. My power is my own.

Our pillow talk is an organic cultivation of safe space that leads us to negative spaces on the days where being black is at the top of my personal hierarchy and Danny unknowingly steps on a racial landmine. Like the time when he asked why black people think whites are responsible for all their misfortune.

"I don't think that's true." Danny says.

"Why do you think black people care about your opinion?" I ask.

"Well, black people are always talking about the white man keeping them down..."

I cut him off before pillow talk becomes a warzone without treaty.

"Who are these black people you know who say they're being held down by whites? I don't know if you've noticed but many of us live well, I do...and I'm black."

We stare.

"I mean...do you know these black people personally, or are you talking about stories from the news or a tv show?" I push gently, nonchalantly.

Danny is visibly cool, but his energy is shook. He sighs, staring at the ceiling fan. I stare at the fan too, remembering the time we went to an all black birthday party at a friend's house in her gated community and Danny made a big deal out of her being black and living in such a big home. I smirk about how half of the people rolled their eyes at me for bringing *whitey*. Especially after he told some sort of a racist sex joke to the guys at the party. Danny snaps out of his trance.

He says, "Your daddy would like me."

I say quickly and assuredly, "No he would not."

"People always like me," Danny says dismissing my clarity.

"Old white men may be racist, but old black men can be quite bitter, especially having to pretend to be okay with whites no matter how poor the treatment. My dad was there for *whites only* signs. Believe me, he would not like you, but... he may tolerate you for his baby girl."

Danny goes silent again.

In this brief pause I contemplate reparations. I know how to ask the right questions to deflate a weak argument, but I would be lying if I'd say Danny didn't have a point. While I have rarely heard any black people around me say, "the white man is holding me back". I have sat in and around lengthy generational tribunals where the discussion of reparations is front and center. I would listen as a teenager and think, *apologies or money wouldn't make a difference to me, I can earn my own money. I can buy my own forty acres and a mule, just get out of my way and watch.* But as I grew older, it occurred to me that many blacks desire the gift of identity, of belonging, a connection to existing in wholeness before slavery. The love/hate many blacks have for America is buried deeply in the cultural wound of lacking identity. Rarely feeling at home or welcome. The perpetual visitor.

My version of reparations is a free DNA clinic for all African-Americans. People don't like feeling lost or orphaned, and black Americans are no different. Many desire connection with their ancestral bodies on a primal level even if they don't know it. A people in limbo, or as W.E.B. DuBois so eloquently stated we contended with, "the double soul of the American negro."

I look over at Danny. I know everything I'm thinking will feel like an attack on him and his ancestors, so I leave my thoughts about reparations in my head. For now.

During pillow talk I wonder if I am letting him slide because of his whiteness? *Am I allowing the exotic nature of our relationship outweigh my very basic relationship deal breakers?* The newness is wearing off and the reality of the relationship is sets in. I don't want to, but I compare my life to those of my friends. They gush over their men, they complain about their men. This reality seems like remnants of another lifetime for me. I don't know how to make men that important anymore. Every conversation is about men, but they have little career interest. I think, *well anyone can make a raggedy old regular man seem golden, I've had and released that opportunity several times over, but a career, a career is yours, a career is your mark, your legacy, your blood sweat and tears.* Then the feminist in me remembers that not all women want a legacy, many are thrilled with simply having a man; even a regular one. I like having a man, but I *love* being successful. If not intellectually, Danny intuitively knows this.

After pillow talk, I strong-arm my orgasm. I push and pull as if I'm trying to rid myself of any desire to come second place to a man just for the sake of having one. He is putty in my hands. I am in a near demonic trance, I hear nothing, I see nothing, I feel everything. My senses are dulled except for my sense of touch. I am touched through my vagina and touched deeper at my core. I vibrate with freedom and ecstasy. I control the thrust, the rhythm, the pace. *I* say when this is over. He is here but I am filling up the space. Every inch of this act embodies my desire. I am in control. I choose all of this. I chose him in this moment. And when I'm ready to no longer choose him, he will be gone. This is the best love we've ever made, and I have no desire for more. It is my love that is sustaining this performance. I am complete. Our experience is complete. This act in my journey is finished.

JAMEELAH RAOOF

CHAPTER TWENTY-6

Something for Nothing

Isn't it funny how mainstream America acts as if ghetto folks invented the lust for money, drugs and sex? Isn't it also funny how all mainstream black images have been created by non-blacks? And isn't it also funny that mainstream America both imitates and alienates black culture, but of course the black culture that it has, itself, framed? It's such a circular game we play. As black Americans we defend our culture when its being appropriated or when it's under attack, but in all honesty, we never created the representations of the black culture that we so vehemently are attached to. It's just so funny...isn't it? Okay, I'm high...but I'm sure you get how much sense I'm making.

I bring these ideas into my classroom. Subtly of course, I realize that being a black woman, I cannot beat the dead horse of racism without being clever, nonchalant and crafty. I began to walk through the social barriers chart I created to show privilege in America. Even though I feel being born in America is a privilege in and of itself, but some do fare better than others. I explain to the students that there are three main indicators of privilege in this country; race, income, and education. I explain to them that these are not my rules but the direct result of our historical values. I explain to them that the least privileged people in this country are brown, poor and uneducated. I explain to them that you can't be all three and be of any value in this country. I explain to them that we can marry across these barriers or attain one of the three to live a better life. Since we can't change our race, people of color have few options; marry white, create a business or become independently wealthy. Or marry someone who has created a business or become independently wealthy. Or become educated or marry someone who is educated. I think, *is this what I am doing?* After all, no matter how much we try to get outside of our programming, we are just like computers. We can only operate within the realms of the software we are given. We may seek new software, but it is always gathered through the lenses in which we have been formed. We escape this programming by reading books, traveling, stepping outside of comfort zones, meditating, etc. But truly, the core, the core is created long before we ever realize what it is made of. As I stand before the students, I contemplate whether my attraction to white men has been programmed. They are enthralled. Their obsession with race has been handed to them, just as my generation and those before mine. I think, *am I using every advantage I can find to catapult over, under, around and through these societal barriers that have been thrusted upon me?* I see freedom in my education from these barriers, I see freedom in being an independent author from these barriers and as I speak, I realize that it is quite possible that I see freedom in dating white to gain even more freedom from these barriers. This is the first time I consider this. I am standing in front of the classroom having an epiphany.

I read once that some black folks in America choose to ignore race because they don't want race to be the underlining issue at the core of their problems. I would go further to say that it's not that many black folks don't want it to be, the fact is, many educated black folks already know that race is an issue at the core of many of their problems, but they choose to ignore it when they realize holding onto that narrative will only hold them back. If they can place all their success on the merit of their own hard work, this gives them back their power. Race is powerless. and determination is powerful. Even if you are forced to prove yourself everywhere you go, it just makes you smarter, stronger and my favorite...better.

People are allowed to think how they think, feel how they feel and act how they act. It is not my quest to change perceptions of me. People must decide if their beliefs limit their love or facilitate its growth. The weight of my own belief system is far too heavy to add the burden of beliefs for random individuals. White spaces have been converted into golden spaces, life spaces, God spaces, my spaces. Everywhere I go I take me with me. I take my beauty, my grace, my kindness and my compassion. I take Yasminah and all the infinite vivaciousness that entails. She is golden. She is enough.

I contemplate self-love in the wee hours of the morning. I cultivate the ability to see myself as a black woman first because I understand that this is the way much of the world sees me first. This is not unfortunate, this is my fortune. I'm okay with being black first and everything else second, because black for me first represents resilience, beauty, triumph, love, courage, grace, strength, truth, magic and brilliance. To look at my black is to see all of that first. All spaces are God spaces and in God spaces I am me. I am every bit of my own story and every bit of my ancestor's stories. Nothing added, and nothing taken away. Perfection.

I am the stack, stacking feels exhausting, not exhilarating, not better. Being just me feels better. Filling my own space feels better, developing my own prairie land feels better, loving everything I am and everything that comes with feels so infinitely better. I can breathe. Not because that cube of stories isn't being hurled at me everywhere I go but because I catch it, hug it, love it, make peace with it and gently place it beside me. I release it. No more standing on top of it. Trying to smother it and trample it. That cube requires its own space just as much as I do.

I embrace white spaces and embrace the discomfort they advance inside of me.

Racism may be one of the symptoms of a nation holding so much diversity, but racism is not the core issue. The core issue is the "something for nothing" foundation upon which my country was built and continues to operate according to. Attaining this great land was something for nothing, slavery was something for nothing, the idea that black men were not real men was just another effort to continue to get something for nothing. *"If they are animals, then free, forced labor wasn't so bad after all...we did them a favor."* The idea that blacks in America should be over the past that has continued to influence their options as citizens today, is a "something for nothing" attitude. A culture of living for today, no consequences, take what you want and pay later, is the problem. White spaces are just a symptom of the something for nothing attitude, the entitlement attitude; even if by chance, white spaces are oblivious to their own entitlement.

But let's be honest, in the age of rampant information technology, there isn't anything a group of people cannot learn about another if they really want to. But instead the something for nothing culture leads them to believe their social, economic, and political privilege has been gained through all their own hard work, diligence and focus. The fact that much prosperity was built on the backs of those Native Americans who were slaughtered and swept aside, the migrant Mexican population who are consistently used for their cheap labor and then threatened with deportation at political convenience, or the black Americans who continue to be the country's scapegoat in all matters concerning immorality and crime, does not occur to many. It definitely does not occur to Danny.

While racism does rear its ugly head, its more obvious to *others* who are constantly tasked with retelling their stories in white spaces; doing their best not to fit the stereotypes that white spaces have created. If you are not white, you are an *other*. The true American crime is entitlement. Therefore, we have overrun prisons and lower and working classes that still need government assistance to survive, regardless of their race. America has yet to learn how to flourish without cashing in on the future and utilizing free and cheap labor to make ends meet. White spaces are just a symptom of her unwavering entitlement, cultivated through the capitalization of non-material cultural expressions of freedom, democracy, whiteness and power.

JAMEELAH RAOOF

ABOUT THE AUTHOR

Jameelah is the mother of two insanely intelligent and beautiful young ladies. She holds an associate's degree in information technology, a bachelor's in mass communication, a master's in information systems management and a master's in applied sociology. She is currently pursuing a PhD in Sociology. She has written and independently published seven books. Jameelah was also recently published as an expert on race and ethnicity in the college text book, "Sociological You". Her next book, "Inequality: A Complete Critique", is set to be released in June of 2020. She has a popular Facebook page, where she enjoys an extensive following and shares motivational tools and insights. Jameelah also owns and operates her own publishing house, JamRa Books, LLC, where she provides online writing workshops for aspiring authors. Her favorite books of all time are, As A Man Thinketh (James Allen), The Science of Getting Rich (Wallace D. Wattles) and The Alchemist (Paulo Cohelo).